About th

Kamakshi Pappu Murti is a professor of German Studies. When she retired a decade ago, she turned her hand to fictional writing. *Murders Most Matronly* (2017) introduced Leela and Meena Rao, two elderly South Asian women whose ambition is to emulate Christie's Jane Marple. *Murders in the Ivory Tower* brings Leela and Meena to the scene of multiple crimes.

Murti has also written children's books, the first of which — *Lalli's Window* — was published

in 2017 by Austin Macauley in Great Britain. Her scholarly writing is devoted to multi-cultural issues, as well as gender studies. Monographs include *India: The Seductive and Seduced 'Other' of German Orientalism* (2000) and *To Veil or not to Veil: Europe's Shape-shifting 'Other'* (2012). Follow her on Facebook, Twitter, and Instagram.

Murti's collection of short stories, *Bandilanka's Forgotten Lives*, is scheduled to be published this year by Leadstart in India.

Murti is presently working on a series about two teens, Yasemin and Nirmala, who navigate peer pressure, social media, and their own physical disabilities.

MURDERS IN THE IVORY TOWER

KAMAKSHI MURTI

MURDERS IN THE IVORY TOWER

Vanguard Press

VANGUARD PAPERBACK

© Copyright 2021
Kamakshi Murti

A CIP catalogue record for this title is
available from the British Library.

ISBN 978 1 80016 171 9

*Vanguard Press is an imprint of
Pegasus Elliot MacKenzie Publishers Ltd.*
www.pegasuspublishers.com

First Published in 2021

**Vanguard Press
Sheraton House Castle Park
Cambridge England**

Printed & Bound in Great Britain

Dedication

For my three parents:
Aunt Lalitha (1919-1979)
My father (1910-1982)
My mother (1917-1994)

Acknowledgements

It is a daunting task to acknowledge by name all the people who have inspired me and helped me craft this tale of two elderly women, Leela and Meena, whose retirement from the humdrum routine of working for a living gave them a new and exciting lease on life.

My childhood was defined by two mothers: my mother, Manikyam, and my paternal aunt, Lalitha. Aunt Lalitha taught me the consequence of education. By achieving the highest educational standard, she became the cornerstone for my own success in the academic world. And my mother, Manikyam, imperceptibly changed our mother-daughter relationship to that of Best Friends Forever.

Without the constant support of every member of my family in Maharashtra, Ohio, Tamilnadu, and Virginia, cousins Leela and Meena would be rushing around in my brain, frustratedly looking for an escape route!

Prologue: 534 BCE, Lumbini, Nepal

Do we have the power to stop a bird from flying?

Whether 'tis nobler in
the mind to suffer...

Prince Siddhartha strode through the corridors of Ramya, one of the three palaces his father, King Suddhodana, had built for his much-loved son. Confined to the delights that the palaces offered, the prince would not be troubled by morbid thoughts about mortality. Ramya meant 'charming' and indeed the palace was delightful in every way.[1] The gilded pillars were adorned with golden vines and silver birds. The corridors opened out to a magical park studded with fish ponds and all manner of exotic blooms.

The heady scent of jasmine kept out the stench of rot beyond the palace grounds that would most certainly offend the delicate nostrils of the prince. Hundreds of crushed rose petals covered the marble tiles to prevent the prince's lotus feet from being scarred. Two courtiers

---

[1] Charming, Very Charming, and Auspicious (Ramya, Suramya, and Subha) for the residence of the young prince, Siddhartha

11

followed the prince as did several slaves gently waving fans of peacock feathers. In the distance, the Himalayas rose into the heavens. But the magnificence of the mountains did not stir any emotions in Siddhartha. He looked at them as if they were outgrowths on a distant planet. His mind was a tabula rasa. The king, his father, had no intention of filling it with knowledge about the outside world.

A black bird suddenly flew out of a nearby honeysuckle bush. It seemed to be hurt and flopped around with its wing extended, going further away from the bush. Suddenly, it flew straight up and let out a call of alarm. Siddhartha followed it with curious eyes, observing the bird's wings, wondering what it would be like to have a pair himself. One of the courtiers, Pasenadi by name, took out his bow and shot an unerring arrow into the bird. It let out a cry and fell to the ground — the arrow staunching the flow of blood. The prince stood rooted to the ground. Why wasn't the bird moving? Had a mere arrow brought it down to earth? Before he could go closer to the dead bird, Pasenadi ordered one of the slaves to pick it up and throw it away. Siddhartha went up to the honeysuckle bush and peered inside. A cup-shaped nest with five bluish-green eggs marked with reddish-brown blotches met his eyes.

That evening, he entered his father's bedchamber. King Suddhodana was lying on a divan, smoking a hookah and being fanned by slaves. A female slave constantly sprayed rose-scented water on the tiles to mitigate the heat of summer.

"Father!" Siddhartha bowed. "Forgive this intrusion, but I saw something today that I could not comprehend. Only your wisdom can enlighten me."

The king sat up, dismissed the slaves, and beckoned to his beloved son to sit next to him.

"Why is my son troubled? Are you not happy? Do we not fulfil your every wish, your every desire?"

"Father!" the prince protested. "I am happy. You have given me my beautiful wife, Yasodharā, and she in turn has given our family my son Rahula. I could not be happier."

"I am pleased to hear that, my son. But those lines of worry on your brow — they are still there."

Siddhartha opened the satchel hanging from his belt. A dead bird with an arrow through its heart lay inside. He had followed the slave and ordered her to give it to him.

"What is this?" the king cried, jumping up from the divan. "What are you doing with... With this bird?"

"Father, I have never seen anything like this before. One moment, the bird was moving, flying. The next moment, it fell down. Pasenadi had merely pierced its body with his arrow. It is now as cold as a stone. Do we have the power to stop a bird from flying? Does Pasenadi have such power?"

King Suddhodana hid his consternation, smiled, and laid a hand on his son's head.

13

"Son, remain in the palaces I have built for you! This is your world, your universe. You are a prince. The bird is of no consequence."

"But... But... Father! If Pasenadi shoots an arrow into me, will I also fall down on the ground and become as cold as stone? Am I then of no consequence?"

Vermont, present day

February 26: Stowe Mountain Lodge hosts a dinner

The board in the lobby of the prestigious Stowe Mountain Lodge in Stowe, Vermont, announced:

Tamarack Ballroom
Hosted by McMoran Advisors International
6:30 p.m. – 10:00 p.m. Cocktails and dinner.
Vice-president Claude Simmons
&
Board of Directors
Guests are requested to use the escalator to the second floor.

Assistant Professor Madhu Trivedi stepped into the grandiose lobby of the hotel and took off her down coat. She tightly draped around her already tense body the red Kanchipuram[2] sari with the purple border that she had thought appropriate for the occasion. She looked around

---

[2] A type of sari traditionally made by weavers from Kanchipuram located in Tamil Nadu, India. These are woven naturally. The Kanchipuram sari is distinguished by its wide contrast borders.

for familiar faces. The words of department head Christopher Reay still rang in her head: "I hope to see each and every one of you tomorrow night at the McMoran event." It was as good as a command. She was a junior faculty member at Anderson College, and consequently, the lowest on the totem pole. McMoran was one of the biggest donors to the College. It offered scholarships to sophomores and juniors who focused on sales, marketing, and management in the communications field with stipends ranging from $3000 to $5000. Even her own department had benefited, albeit through one-time funding of a lecture by an internationally known scholar of media theory.

A commissionaire came up to Madhu, glanced at the invite she held in her hands, and imperiously waved a gold-braided uniformed arm in the direction of the escalator. Madhu suppressed an urge to giggle, waved her thanks with an equally supercilious arm, and sailed almost as magnificently as the commissionaire towards the escalator. Her mimicry of pompous politicians and other personages had always got a laugh from relatives and friends. It could very well get her into trouble.

Chandeliers blinded Madhu as she entered the Tamarack Ballroom. She headed for the bar and got herself a glass of sweet lemonade. She didn't mind the occasional glass of Merlot or Malbec, but she didn't enjoy drinking alone. The entire college administration, including her department head, would be present. She spotted Professor Gayatri Sullivan-Mehra, a full professor in the Socio-Anthropology Department, and heaved a sigh of relief. She had chosen Anderson College mainly because of this woman who was a leading scholar on Muslim immigration to Europe and the United States.

"Professor Sullivan-Mehra!"

Sullivan-Mehra turned around. For this evening's event, she had put on a jet-black silk caftan. Her short-spiked hair was coloured a brilliant henna red. She towered a good six inches over Madhu's five foot three. But there was not a hint of arrogance in the luminous black eyes that were now directed at this junior faculty member.

"Ah yes! I remember! Christopher sent me your CV. Very impressive. Trivedi, right? Madhu."

"Yes, Professor Sullivan-Mehra. Good memory. It's a real privilege!"

Sullivan-Mehra laughed and took a sip of red wine.

"Call me Gayatri. Well, what do you think?" she said, waving her hand at the crowd. "All this 'pride, pomp, and circumstance...'! I must confess, I don't share Othello's enthusiasm for such ceremonies."

She looked around.

"Have to admit, though, that ultimately networking has its advantages, especially when the board members of McMoran are 'mingling'! The college can always use more money. By the way, the McMorans are the ones with those purple and red badge ribbons."

Madhu saw a tall, handsome man in an expensively tailored suit talking with Christopher Reay. She could see the ribbon on the man's lapel. Typical of Christopher, my honourable department head, she thought. He doesn't waste much time kissing ass.

"Madhu," Gayatri broke into her thoughts, "I'm scheduled to visit your class in a couple of weeks. I always like to be prepared before such visits. It helps me, and I'm sure it helps the person under review. Could you send me a copy of your syllabus?"

"Yes, of course. I was planning to do so this week. If you need any other materials…"

"No. The review committee has lots of documentation. I just needed to know exactly what you would be teaching that day. And one other thing — I know we are there to observe, not to participate. But occasionally, especially when a discussion is flagging, I like to pose a question or two."

"That would be fantastic! Of course — please do so. It would help lessen the anxiety my students feel when senior faculty sit silently behind them."

Before they could continue the conversation, Christopher Reay had latched on to Gayatri. Madhu saw a petite redhead engage the good-looking man in conversation. Reay's voice burst in on them:

"Gayatri, my dear! You look absolutely ravishing! Let me get you some more wine."

In his eagerness, he almost stumbled over Madhu.

"Excuse me! Ah, Madhu. Good to see you here. You have your native costume on, I see."

"And you yours, Christopher," Gayatri interjected.

Madhu once again had a hard time suppressing a giggle.

"And do get both of us some red, if you would. My preference is for a Malbec. What is yours, Madhu?"

What the heck! Madhu thought, throwing caution to the wind. She realized that she had a powerful ally in Gayatri. Old Christopher could lump it.

"I'll have the same."

Dinner was spectacular, quite unlike the rubber chicken and wilted salad that most academic conferences were condemned to eat. From the spiced olives, the scallop and cucumber soup, to the saffron risotto with chicken and asparagus in a parmesan shell, the meal was a gourmet's dream. And when she was convinced that she couldn't take another bite, a miraculous tiramisu appeared on the table. She had managed to get seated next to Gayatri, and they held a stimulating whispered conversation throughout the inevitable long, dreary speeches that each board member felt obliged to give.

An exhilarated Madhu hurriedly got into her car, brought around by a valet, and switched on the heat. Vermont in February could freeze one's blood. She was about to drive off when there was a tap on the window.

"Pardon the intrusion!" a deep husky voice with a decidedly Etonian accent said. "I hope I'm not too late."

She looked up, irritation written all over her face. She remembered her five-year spell at the University of Oxford that a Rhodes scholarship had made possible. Her father, an Etonian himself, had never quite shaken off his perceived allegiance to a colonial ruler, forgetting that his 'fellow' Etonians had tolerated him as a Brown Sahib, recreating the opaque ceiling that separated them from him.[3] Hers had been a so-called post-colonial time, but the ceiling had been exchanged for more transparent material — like glass. There had been no scarcity of Etonians among her batch mates. She wondered how this black man had fared. It was the same tall handsome man whom Christopher Reay had collared earlier on. She wound her window down a crack.

"Yes?"

He smiled and slipped her his card through the crack.

"Charles, Charles Nandoro. My misfortune that I did not have the opportunity to meet you earlier tonight. Professor Trivedi, I am interested in your research — on

---

[3] 'Brown sahib': a term used to refer to natives of South Asia who imitate Western—typically English—lifestyle. It is also used to refer to those have been heavily influenced by Western—usually British—culture and thinking. It is mostly used as a derogatory term. By implication, a Brown Sahib goes beyond simply mimicking the Western lifestyle. A Brown Sahib will usually have an unfair bias towards West vis-à-vis East.

immigration, I believe. As an immigrant myself, I would very much like to discuss your research further. May I call on you at Anderson?"

Smooth! she thought. Very smooth! Knows my name, knows about my research. This is too weird! Wonder what he wants. On the other hand, networking — that's what Gayatri called it. Well, I can network as well as anyone else, especially if good looks and charm are part of the process.

"Thank you, Mr.... Er... Nandoro. Very kind. But please call ahead of time."

She smirked and quickly rolled up the window before Nandoro could continue. As she drove away, she thought she detected similar amusement in his eyes.

March 15: Madhu's annoying avatar

One of his students asked Buddha,
"Are you the messiah?"
"No," answered Buddha.
"Then are you a healer?"
"No," Buddha replied.
"Then are you a teacher?" the student persisted.
"No, I am not a teacher."
"Then what are you?" asked the student, exasperated.
"I am awake," Buddha replied.

(Buddha)

I, also, would like to look
and smile, sit and walk like that,
so free, so worthy, so restrained,
so candid, so childlike and mysterious.
A man only looks and walks like that
when he has conquered his Self.
I also will conquer my Self…
No other teachings will attract me,
since this man's teachings have not done so.

(Hermann Hesse)

"No other teachings will attract me, since this man's teachings have not done so" — the condescension was palpable. It was quintessential Hesse, glossing over the Buddha's words to the question: "Are you a teacher?"

"I am awake!" The words resonated. That was the essence of the Buddha — awake to possibilities, willing to overcome egoistic posturing. Madhu posted both quotes on the listserv for her seniors. *Let them ponder the words! It may very well turn out to be the cornerstone of the course.* Two hours later, she stood up from her desk in the lecture hall, closed her laptop, shoved it into her briefcase, and announced: "I expect your assignments to be in my mailbox by five p.m. today. Any submission later than that — well, you know my policy."

She was about to pick up a sponge to wipe down the whiteboard, but Sean O'Flaherty beat her to it. The black-haired, green-eyed junior smiled ingratiatingly. Females didn't take long to swoon over him, he told himself. He desperately needed to get at least a B in this course if he wanted to maintain his athletic scholarship. But this bitch was proving impossible to bend to his obvious charms.

"Thank you."

"Anything else I can do for you, Professor, anything at all?"

He never stops, she thought with disgust, remembering a day the previous week when he had stormed into her office. He had let out a howl of anguish, knelt down at her feet, and wound his arms around her legs, begging her to take pity on him. She had always disliked melodrama. On stage, she would have applauded Sean's performance as a commendable charade of the genre. She had pushed him away, slapped him hard, and threatened to call security.

She suppressed a shudder, zipped her briefcase shut, and looked at him.

"Yes, Sean. You could finish your assignment on time — for a change."

She noted with satisfaction the scowl on his face as she marched out of the hall. Later that evening, she walked back to her office, her mind full of how she would prepare for the next day's courses. She sat down wearily at her desk. Assignments were piling up on her already cluttered desk. Seniors and juniors alike had finally realized that any delay meant a lower grade. She had no patience for procrastination. She slowly picked up the topmost paper in the pile from her capstone course for seniors on the German writer Hermann Hesse. The bolded title made her smile: "Homoeroticism in Hesse's *Siddhartha*." Things had looked very different two years ago.

Two years ago, she had nervously sat in the 'electric chair' at the annual conference of American Sociology and Anthropology in San Francisco. Not surprisingly, she had received more than a dozen letters calling her for interviews at the conference site. She had held unusual cards and had had no qualms about using them to her advantage. She could almost hear the department heads and chairs looking at her curriculum vitae and ticking off the categories: "older, i.e., non-traditional = check; a woman = check; a woman of colour = check; a woman from a non-European culture = check; experience in teaching diversity = check." One of her acquaintances had told her not to wear Asian-Indian clothing to the interviews. But she had resisted a dress code dictated by a Eurocentric business world just to get a job.

"If they equate a woman clad in clothes of her choice with ignorance or backwardness, that is their problem, not mine," she had indignantly retorted. "How I choose to dress shouldn't be the topmost concern of an educational institution."

She had donned an ankle-long printed cotton skirt that she had picked up on her last trip to India, and a black silk shirt. A colourful dupatta[4] had draped her shoulders. She knew that the silver jewellery she had added would also be seen as exotic. Any department that found her appearance distasteful was not for her. As far as knowledge went, she was sure most of the interviewers would know less about her research than she did. That confidence brought her nine campus interviews followed by eight tenure-track offers.

She suddenly choked as her eyes fell on a silver-framed photograph on her desk. It showed her with her parents, taken during happier times — her childhood. Long-suppressed memories of a brutal murder flooded

---

[4] A long, multi-purpose scarf.

her mind now, memories of the murder of her mother, Komal Trivedi, five years ago in Tucson, Arizona. She had almost died of grief and despair. Her father had succumbed to cancer the previous year. Although Madhu had moved away soon after to work at the Marriott in Minnesota as an accountant, the daily call to her mother had helped both of them work through their grief. But in the wake of her mother's violent death, she had desperately felt the need for a surrogate womb into which she could crawl. Friends had provided that haven. She had finally managed to breathe through the trauma. Two of her best friends, the Kalluris — Bureau Chief Murali Kalluri worked at the Tucson Police Department, and his wife Meghna Kalluri was a practicing counselling psychologist, volunteering a couple of evenings at the South Tucson Youth Center — had persuaded her to try something different, perhaps even to go back to school. She had done just that. She had enrolled in the graduate interdisciplinary program of Comparative Cultural and Literary Studies, filled with trepidation at her re-entry into student life.

She was a good ten years older than her classmates. But her colleagues were quite oblivious to her age. And the four years of intense intellectual stimuli that her doctoral work provided gave back to her the sense of purpose that she had lost for a while.

Madhu had chosen Anderson College only because of Gayatri Sullivan-Mehra. It had been a difficult decision for Madhu, taking her far away from Tucson.

She thought of the two women to whom she fondly referred as 'Leela aunty' and 'Meena aunty'. They were not just close family friends. The cousins had helped Madhu's childhood friend, Murali, catch the serial killer responsible for her mother's death, and had formed part of the tight circle keeping her safe from her demons. Leela aunty had stood by her through the anxiety-ridden period of applying for jobs. As a full professor of Cognitive and Behavioural Psychology at the University of Arizona, Leela Rao had plenty of experience interviewing Ph.D. candidates for entry-level positions. She had even held mock interviews with Madhu.

"Two years!" Madhu thought. She found the students at Anderson College intellectually challenging, open to new ideas. And her colleagues were interesting for the most part. What left her frustrated was the content of the courses the department head forced upon her. By reason of her heritage, she became the designated teacher of all things South-Asian, although her doctoral thesis had been on Black Muslim feminism in the US, with a minor in comparative religions. She was born and bred in the U.S., but try as she might, she couldn't shake off the assumption of India/Yoga/spirituality that her appearance provoked everywhere she went.

"Hesse, the Guru from Calw, Germany!" she mused. Very few scholars knew that the German poet had rejected twentieth-century India because of an aversion to something that had not crossed his path: unromanticized poverty. Hastily skirting India, he had cautiously ventured into Sri Lanka and select isles in the Indonesian archipelago before inventing his very own Avatar: a Protestant Buddha. That first semester at the college, Madhu had offered the students interpretations of Hesse consecrated by older Germanists, hating herself all the while for not being more honest, yet fearing repercussions if she revealed her inner maverick so soon. To her dismay, when the department chair saw enrolments jump, he asked her to teach Hesse again, adding that it would 'add an important dimension to your portfolio'. An Assistant Professor rarely argued with the department head, especially in view of her imminent third-year review. But she could at least frame the course differently. She encouraged the students to research and compare various religious systems, laying emphasis on the nontheistic belief system that was Buddhism. She knew the kinds of questions that would surface in discussions about Hesse's writings.

She leafed through some more papers. *The Seductive Power of Hermann Hesse, Women in Hesse's Oeuvre, Was Hesse gay? Hesse's worry: To enlighten or not to enlighten!"* She smiled. Yes, the chair had required her to stand in front of Hesse's faux Bodhi[5] tree, and yes, she had been forced to don the psychedelic

---

[5] According to Buddhist texts the Buddha, after his Enlightenment, spent a whole week in front of the Bodhi tree.

robes of a mythical India that the Timothy Learys[6] of the world had devised for her. But she was damned if she was going to lead her students up the garden path of instant Nirvana! They would have to seek out the Hermann Hessian mantel of pseudo-religiosity elsewhere. One of the members of the review committee would be visiting her nine o'clock class "The Brothers Grimm and other tales of horror" that she had cross-listed with several departments. She would have to guard her tongue.

A member of the review committee had attended her Hesse course the previous week. She had briefly considered prostituting herself and presenting a reading of Hesse more palatable to the member, knowing that he was one of those card-carrying baby boomers who had cried 'flower-power' in the '60s and most probably kept a well-thumbed pocket edition of Siddhartha in his kurtha. But as quickly she had dismissed the idea. Goethe and Hesse. The eighteenth-century German poet had driven his youthful audience to despair and suicide with his novel *The Sorrows of Young Werther*. The twentieth-century German 'Buddha' had convinced his young readers that his brand of Nirvana was the ultimate panacea for their despair.

---

[6] LSD was popularized in the 1960s by individuals such as psychologist Timothy Leary, who encouraged American students to "turn on, tune in, and drop out." This created an entire counterculture of drug abuse and spread the drug from America to the United Kingdom and the rest of Europe.

The committee member had remained seated after Madhu had dismissed the class. He had been appalled at her "complete disregard for the intellectual prowess of one of the greats of German literature."

"Young lady," he had patronizingly chided her, possibly still wallowing in those LSD-tinted countercultural dreams of the '60s, "you people should be more aware of the spiritual heritage that ancient India possessed. It took a philosopher like Hermann Hesse to reveal those riches to you. And now you reject his wisdom with such hauteur?"

'Hauteur'? Really? With what arrogant ease he managed to use the word! And 'you people' put her in her place, didn't it? How dare she as a young woman from a former colonized, now 'third-world' country critique a seer like Hesse? Three strikes and you're out: woman, colonized, third-world. Well, there go my chances of tenure, she thought bitterly. Once again, the West had interpreted for the East what the latter ostensibly didn't understand about itself.

A knock on the door woke her up from these unhelpful thoughts.

"Professor, I... I..."

Madhu recognized the voice of her brightest student. A mop of red hair became visible, followed by the bashful face and lanky body of the teen. Martin McDonald slipped into the office, hiding his oversized, rather moist hands behind his back.

"I wondered… That is, did you get to… I mean… Get to see my paper?"

"'Homoeroticism in Hesse's Siddhartha.' I find the title intriguing. I'm sure the content will be equally thought-provoking."

Martin's mouth widened into a huge smile.

"Thank you, Professor. S… Sorry for the intrusion."

He turned and awkwardly ran out. Nalini heard a male voice greeting him.

"Hey, Mart! Dropped your apple… And your three-dollar bill!"[7]

She heard raucous laughter and caught a glimpse of a red-faced Martin disappearing down the corridor before her door swung shut.

"Kids are brutal," she thought. She knew that the mocking voice belonged to Sean O'Flaherty, the same Sean whose slimy attempts to curry favor with her always ended badly for him. Sean's spectacular performance on the soccer field had got him a full scholarship. But the punishing grades she had given him in her courses had recently brought the college coach rushing to her door.

"You need to understand, Professor… Eh… Trivedi. He is a star athlete, brought us three straight wins. He has to maintain a B average to keep his scholarship. And he has Bs in all the other courses. But

---

[7] A euphemism for homosexuality.

your grades are bringing the average down to a C. I cannot for the life of me figure out why you insist on giving him such poor grades."

"Coach Miller, I don't insist on anything, only on a commitment to education and hard work. I give him the grades he deserves," she had retorted. "Perhaps you could persuade him to concentrate more on his studies? After all, this is an academic institution."

The red-faced coach had stormed out. A half-hour later, she had received an email from the Dean of Students about the importance of supporting 'our athletes'.

"Madhu, I would urge you to provide as much assistance as possible to Sean. I am sure you are well aware that the very fate of intercollegiate athletics at our institution depends on Sean's continued success on the field. Perhaps some judicious tutoring or an independent study might be more helpful than merely handing out bad grades. Best, Hugh."

"Pompous ass!" she had thought, bristling at the reprimand. She would not compromise academic integrity for the sake of a steroid-pumped body with a brain the size of a pea.

"Hugh, I'm sure you will understand," she had fired back at the dean, mimicking his tone, "that I cannot treat Sean any differently than my other students. You will agree that we must hold all students to the same standards. I have made every accommodation open to us as teachers without compromising the rigorous criteria of academic excellence to which our college holds us. For example, I have tried to provide remedial help. But Sean has been unable to complete even the classwork that I have assigned. I have also spent considerable time outside of my office hours to discuss each paper, each exam carefully with Sean, and have not failed to give him the option to rewrite some of his assignments. Again, and regrettably, he has never once availed himself of these opportunities to better his performance. Should you wish to discuss the matter in greater detail with me, I would be happy to show you all his assignments so that you may judge for yourself the validity of the grades he has received. Best, Madhu."

She sighed. The satisfaction in imitating his pompous style was short-lived. In the long run, it might very well sound the death-knell to her career at this college, perhaps even in academics. She had basically disobeyed a direct request from the high command. Well, Sean was arrogant and dishonest. He was known to intimidate classmates into doing his research for him, sometimes even into writing some of his assignments for him. But she had no clear evidence of such fraud except for a couple of B's he had miraculously achieved.

She picked up Martin's paper and was soon absorbed in the astonishingly beautiful prose of this well-researched paper.

March 15: A macabre turn of events

"When you encounter
the unbelievers on the
battle-field, strike off their
heads until you have crushed
them completely;
then bind the prisoners tightly."

[Sura 47:3]

He read through the letter he had just printed out. F***! That didn't sound right. He'd have to change it, reprint it. Now! That's better, should do the trick. The fag-hag won't last much longer here. He got up, stuck the letter and something else into an envelope, and shoved it into one of the mailboxes against the side wall. He looked at his watch. There was no time to lose. He hastily picked up his backpack and opened the door.

***

The figure in a hoodie looked carefully around the room. Orders had been explicit. The figure arranged everything carefully, checking a list on a smartphone. It punched in a number on the phone and said: "It's done. …Yes, I'll be there."

Picking up the backpack, the figure opened the French doors and vaulted over the low wall of the balcony onto the lawn.

***

Madhu relaxed in her chair smiling at the three calls she had received. That Etonian accent — she was both drawn to and repelled by it. He was infuriatingly attractive. It was six years since she had last felt like this. He had done his research on her. That was flattering indeed, as was his persistence. Obviously, he wasn't someone who would take 'no' for an answer. She looked at the card he had slipped into her hand outside the Stowe Mountain Lodge.

Charles Nandoro, Vice President
Regional Manager, Northeast
McMoran International Services LLC
Montpelier, VT

Impressive. She tried to silence the South-Asian cultural voice — possibly her grandmother's — that needled her: "He is at the peak of his career and not married? Be careful, girl!" Well, she didn't know about his past. Did it matter? She hadn't met a really interesting man since her divorce ten years ago. That marriage — she had just turned eighteen — had been a big mistake. She had run away with a childhood sweetheart. Within a few months, they had both realized that they had nothing in common except for raging hormones.

She glanced at the card again. Charles Nandoro. An interesting name. She had looked it up, looked him up. She came up with several hits on the internet. He was from Zimbabwe, migrated as a child to the UK with parents and siblings. Madhu wondered what the name meant. Bottom line, she would be spending a stimulating evening with a very good-looking, sophisticated man. And he had suggested one of the more expensive restaurants in the city. Good food, good company. What more did one need?

She glanced at her watch. Time to go home, prepare for the next day's classes, and then spend an enjoyable couple of hours choosing something nice to wear for the evening. Wow! She felt as if she were preparing for a first date. Well, her life hadn't left her much time for romance. She opened her briefcase to make sure she hadn't forgotten her notes. Her hand came up empty. Where are they? I can't walk into the classroom without them, not this time. The second member of the review committee will be seated in the back row, ready to trip her up at the first opportunity. God! She was being paranoid. Take a deep breath! she told herself.

She hated doing things off-the-cuff. The notes couldn't have disappeared into thin air. Perhaps she had left them behind in the mailroom where the printer was located. She groaned. If she was lucky, only the interdepartmental administrative assistant, Lucy

Gilmore, would be there. She hurried to the mailroom. The door was locked. She glanced at her watch. It was past six o'clock! Of course, Lucy would have gone for the day. Madhu inserted a key and pushed the door. What's wrong with the damn door? She pushed again, but something was blocking it. Push! She managed to open it a crack. She slid her hand through it and felt on the other side for the obstruction. Nothing so far. She slid her hand further down. Finally, she grabbed something — it felt like hair! Ugh! She quickly removed her hand. It was stained red.

March 16: Professor Leela Rao dons cap and gown

"Don't tell me it's Halloween already!" Meena Rao exclaimed. Her plump cousin, Leela, had just donned her Harvard doctoral gown and cap, and was turning this way and that in front of a full-length mirror.

"Idiot!" Leela laughed. "I've been invited to be the commencement speaker at Anderson College in Vermont — May 18th. See? The robe still fits, all these years later!"

Meena went up to her cousin and turned the cap to a rakish angle.

"Now you look truly dignified — for a clown! And may I remind you that the robe fits only because you have always maintained your… Ahem… Embonpoint?"

"Cut it out!" Leela yelled, pulling the cap back straight again. She examined herself more critically in the mirror. "The robe is rather wrinkled. I suppose I have to iron it!"

Meena grinned.

"Do you even know how to use an iron? Fatso! You have never, not once in your seventy-six years of existence, thought about ironing anything out except perhaps the occasional wrinkle in the only functional organ in your body: the brain. So why this sudden insistence on elegance?"

"You're right," Leela agreed almost too quickly. "I don't really care. It's my speech, my words of inspiration and wisdom that they want, not fashion advice... Oh, stop that silly giggle! Okay, okay! I'll take it to the dry-cleaners. Your superior 'I was a high-powered New York corporate lawyer and you are my country cousin' attitude... You always know which button to push, don't you!"

She took off the robe, crushed it into a bundle, and took out the keys to her beloved VW bug. She stopped on the front veranda of their adobe-style house.

"You want to come along, Meena? It might be fun. From Montpelier, we could drive up to Montreal, do some sightseeing, eat some of those delicious crepes at Juliette & Chocolat..."

She paused.

"What a great place! My lack of French didn't matter, did it? I understood enough to order the best."

Meena giggled again.

"Language never is a barrier for you when your gastronomic juices are flowing!"

She smiled fondly at her cousin.

"You actually remember the name of that place after all these years? You are incredible! And of course, food would somehow be part of this commencement speaker scam of yours!"

Leela said with a sly smile, "My unwrinkled brain needs proper sustenance. And those crepes were truly memorable. The chocolate filling alone — yum!"

"If memory serves, the four of us were there together. What was it? Forty years ago?"

"Yup! You, me, those twin hubbies of ours."

Meena smiled at the recollection of her peeved husband. "I also remember that my poor Arvind hated crepes. He preferred our South-Indian dosais. Kept on about how white people had no idea how to prepare spicy savouries. But the three of us — we more than made up for Arvind's lack of enthusiasm. For once, those identical twins didn't like the same thing!"

"Well," Leela said thoughtfully, "That's not quite true, you know. Dosais are also a kind of crepe, without the egg and milk. So maybe even here our guys were not that different!"

"Before you leave, just toss the newspaper into the room."

Meena got herself a second cup of her delicious Peaberry coffee and managed to dodge the newspaper that came at her like an arrow. As she sat down and opened it, the sounds of a guffaw faded away into the distance. She looked at the headlines of the Arizona Citizen, then quickly skipped to her favourite section, 'News from around the nation.' Her eyes widened as she read one of the items.

Montpelier, VT — March 16: The body of star athlete Sean O'Flaherty was discovered yesterday in the mailroom of the Department of Cultural Studies at the prestigious Anderson College. Death was due to blunt force trauma to the head. O'Flaherty was just two months away from graduating. Police are treating the star quarterback's death as a homicide.

March 16: Headlines

The Vermonter Herald, March 16, 2006

Quarterback O'Flaherty found murdered at Anderson College!

The body of star athlete Sean O'Flaherty was discovered yesterday in the mailroom of the Department of Cultural Studies at the prestigious Anderson College. Death was due to blunt force trauma to the head. O'Flaherty was just two months away from graduating. The athlete's father, Michael O'Flaherty, US Ambassador to Zimbabwe, is presently in the capital Harare. He and his wife have been notified of their son's death and are scheduled to fly back on a special jet. Police are treating the star quarterback's death as a homicide.

***

President Carlos Juarez cleared his throat. He looked at the sea of faces in the assembly hall of the administrative building. This was one of the more painful tasks of his presidency, mourning the death of a member of his community, especially when his life had been taken in such an inhumane fashion.

"Anderson College students, faculty, and staff! It is with deep sadness that I address you today, sadness at the woefully premature loss of a life. This semester ought to have been a joyful time for Sean. He would have graduated in a couple of months. Instead, we are here to mourn his death. We are all in shock, unable to grasp the magnitude of the loss."

He heard sporadic sounds of sobbing.

"Our hearts and prayers go out to Sean's parents and siblings. And now I would like to request a moment's silence in memory of Sean."

After a minute, he cleared his throat and glanced at a piece of paper.

"His family will post visitation hours for Sean at St. Paul's United Methodist Church as soon as the police release his body. Reverend Jonathan Williamson will conduct services."

March 17: A coach lines his pockets

Coach Jeb Miller entered the opulent conference hall of McMoran Advisors International. The executive vice-president, Claude Simmons, was expected any minute to give his usual spiel about the economy and the company as a world leader in its field. Miller took a seat in the back row, close to the door. He looked around. It was not yet time. He'd have to listen to the Simmons guy bullshit for a few minutes. Simmons walked into the hall, followed by half a dozen assistants, each furiously punching numbers and text into their smartphones as he spouted out predictions. Miller groaned. This was a monthly charade he had to undergo. But the payoff was excellent. He had another ten years to go before retirement, and he needed all the greenbacks he could lay his hands on to maintain his mistress in that studio apartment. His wife knew about her and held that knowledge over his head every single day. Theirs had long been a broken marriage. But a divorce would ruin his career — she would take him to the cleaners. Without this monthly payoff, he was a goner.

A man in his mid-forties quietly entered and sat next to Miller. He handed Miller a black cloth bag and a thick envelope. Miller opened the bag and counted a dozen small baggies. He placed the bag and envelope in his duffel bag. As he crept out of the hall, he could hear Simmons droning on about profit margins and sound investments.

March 17: Bloodbath

"It degrades human dignity. It's unnatural,
and there is no question ever of allowing
these people to behave worse than dogs
and pigs... If you see people parading themselves as Lesbians and Gays, arrest them
and hand them over to the police!"

(President Robert Mugabe, Zimbabwe,
on homosexuality, 1 August 1995)

Martin proofed the document one last time. Professor Trivedi had been super thorough in her critique of his paper. He really enjoyed writing for her. Unlike many of the other profs, she made an honest effort to understand his perspective. And this time, she had commended him for courageously entering outlawed territory in Hesse research. Each and every one of her comments felt as if she were engaging in a dialog with him. This was the fourth time he was attending one of her courses.

He hit the print button, carefully placed the twenty-three pages into a plastic folder, and slid the folder into Trivedi's mailbox. He printed a second copy and tucked it into his backpack. He wondered what Ignatius would say. They had been together for six months now. It was in his freshman year that Martin had met Ignatius Munyaradzi during a study abroad program in Harare, Zimbabwe. Ignatius was one of the student reps for the residence hall where Martin roomed. Ignatius had introduced Martin to his Shona family. Within a month of his stay in Harare, Martin had been unofficially inducted into the Shona's belief in an impersonal, omnipotent or principal Creator, called *Muwari*, *Musikavanhu*, or a Spirit which creates good and bad. He had learned how to give thanks to the spirits of the land, the *mhondoro* and ancestors, before eating vegetable leaves, and how to prepare beer from the traditional millet of the Shona for religious ceremonies. He had gained insights into a rich cultural heritage.

The two kept in touch via Instagram and Snapchat after Martin's return to Montpelier. Ignatius had applied for an exchange program and was now in Anderson College attending courses in the Sociology-Anthropology Department. He also received a stipend as a teaching assistant in the African Studies Department.

Martin rode his bike up Cummings Street to the apartment block where the two had rented a studio apartment. He parked his bike in the basement, removed a wheel, and walked with it up to the second floor. He couldn't wait to show Ignatius his paper. It was Ignatius who had seen in Hesse's *Steppenwolf* clear evidence of bisexuality, comparing it to *Death in Venice*, a novel by another German writer Thomas Mann.

Martin placed the bike wheel against the wall and rummaged in his backpack for the house key. Ignatius should be at home, he thought. But with his headphones turned up to full volume, he would never hear knocking on the door. Martin opened the door, slipped, and fell into a pool of red.

***

An officer of the Montpelier Police Force opened the door to Chief Inspector Bonnie Martel's office.

"Just got this from Forensics, Chief. Our officers were searching the building where the Department of Cultural Studies is housed. One of the seniors volunteered the info that a couple of trophies were missing from the department's display cabinet! Apparently, the student had been part of a debating team that had won one of them. She was quite distraught, came running to the officers about a burglary. According to the ME, such a trophy could very well be the murder weapon. The killer didn't have to look far for a weapon — it was easily accessible."

"That's good work, Sergeant."

The phone on Martel's desk rang.

"Chief Inspector Martel. Yes, right away."

She placed the phone back in its cradle.

"We have another homicide. A young Zimbabwean exchange student — Ignatius Munyaradzi. He was living with another student, Martin McDonald. Martin called 911."

As Bonnie Martel entered the studio, she saw a lanky boy with a red mop of hair sitting on an ottoman, face buried in outsized red hands. He looked up at her with eyes red from weeping.

March 17: Forensics discovers things

Sergeant Erickson handed Bonnie Martel a report.

"Martin McDonald?" she asked.

Martin nodded mutely and stood up. His shirt and pants were covered with blood.

"Can I get you anything? A coke? Something else to drink?"

He didn't hear what she said.

"He's… He's gone! My sweet Ignatius… They cut off his head — like a chicken! They…"

He collapsed on the floor, sobs wracking his body. Martel turned to Sergeant Erickson.

"Sergeant, would you please bring him to the station later? See to his needs?"

She addressed the uniforms who had been dispatched by 911.

"What else did you find, officers?"

"His wallet, some loose change, but no cell."

"No cell? Interesting!"

"And the same Arabic calligraphy carved into his chest as in the O'Flaherty case, Chief!"

She winced at the recollection of those letters carved into O'Flaherty's chest as well. The police interpreter had read aloud:

"Al-ḥamdu lillāh" (All Praise and Thanks to Allah):
أُشْكُرُ الله دائِمًا

She turned to the officers. "Go talk to the neighbours; see if anyone witnessed anything unusual."

The ME and his team continued scouring the room for evidence.

***

Martin McDonald sat in one of the interrogation rooms.

He was clad in fresh clothes. Chief Inspector Martel entered and sat opposite him.

"I am Chief Inspector Bonnie Martel. Martin, I have to ask you about your friend. Can you do that?"

Martin nodded mutely.

"Would you tell me in your own words what happened?"

Martin haltingly began with the bike ride home, his excitement about his paper, his search for the house key.

"And I opened the door, stepped inside, and slipped. I raised my face and saw that I was lying on top of..."

He choked and laid his head face down on the table.

Martel pushed a glass of water towards him. He wiped his face and took a sip.

"So much blood... I couldn't stop it. I tried... His head had just... Just rolled to the side. Can you imagine? Like a football." He burst out into hysterical laughter. "Can you believe it? I tried to put it back..."

"Martin, look at me! Look at me! It was N-O-T… Y-O-U-R… F-A-U-L-T!" She spoke slowly and firmly. "You couldn't have prevented it."

"He… I loved him." He burst out, "How could anyone… Did the killer… I mean, was my Ignatius assaulted, sexually I mean?"

"We don't know yet. The ME has to complete his autopsy. Martin, anything you can tell us about who his enemies are, who might have had it in for him?"

"Enemies and Ignatius? He was one of the kindest, most thoughtful people I have ever met. I can't think of him and enemies in the same breath. And he was the most popular TA in the African Studies Department."

Martel stood up.

"Okay. You need to rest now. But we'll have to secure your apartment for a while. Do you have anyone with whom you can stay for a night or two?"

"Yes," Martin replied faintly. "Yes, my friend Sheila."

"Just tell one of the officers outside to take you to her. And Martin, I am truly sorry for your loss. If you remember anything, anything at all, please call me at the station."

"What is it?" the chief asked, as Martin hesitated at the door.

"One more thing. Ignatius belonged to the Shona in Zimbabwe. His parents, his family will want to carry out certain rituals to… To free his spirit. After the autopsy, will his body be… I mean, will he look… All right? The head — his parents shouldn't be allowed to see him like that."

Bonnie Martel saw the lost look in his eyes and grieved. Life was ruthless.

"Usually, we have to get the permission of the legal custodian, in this case, Ignatius' parents. But since we have a homicide…"

Martin winced perceptibly at the use of the word.

Martel continued, "… on our hands, a case with impelling legal implications, our Medical Examiner will need to perform an autopsy. But I will request him to give the… I promise he will treat your friend with the utmost respect in embalming him."

"Embalming? Yes, yes. He'll be sleeping, won't he?"

Bonnie went up to him and laid a comforting hand on his shoulder.

"Yes, he will, Martin — just sleeping."

Martin got up.

"He had so much going for him! He was the first in his family to leave his city, his country."

Martin took out his wallet, looked at a photograph, traced its outlines lovingly with a fingertip, and gently put it back.

"Thank you, Chief Inspector. You've been very kind. I don't know what I'd have done…"

He hobbled to the door like an old man and allowed himself to be led out by an officer. Martel sat down, her heart aching as she watched him. His world had been turned topsy-turvy in the blink of an eye. She asked herself as she did, every single time she was confronted by such violence, why she had chosen this profession. To protect people, to rid the world of monsters, she told herself. But when you begin seeing yourself in the victim, the pain and suffering eat away at you.

March 17/18: Vermont beckons

"We should cancel our trip," Meena Rao said to cousin Professor Leela Rao.

"Not a good idea, Cousin," Leela said, looking at her emails. "Here's one from Madhu. You know, Komal's child, the one who is Assistant Professor at the college. There's been a second murder. An exchange student from Zimbabwe. Madhu seems to be up to her neck in them. She knows we are going there in May, but she'd like us to come right away if we can. She needs our support."

A day later, the cousins stood in the baggage claim area of Burlington International Airport, waiting for their suitcases to appear on the carousel. Leela said, "President Carlos Juarez called me, told me about the two murders, and hurried to assure me that the commencement ceremonies wouldn't be cancelled. They would be held, albeit in a very low-key manner. And he still wants me to speak at commencement. Who would want to kill that boy?"

She looked around the baggage claim area.

"Where is she?" she grumbled, before dropping her plump body onto the nearest chair.

"She must have been delayed," Meena pacified her, knowing her cousin's short fuse, especially after an uncomfortable flight and the crap that airlines served under the label 'snacks' and 'drinks'. "It is five thirty, office traffic. She has to drive all the way from Montpelier. Didn't she mention something about a forty-minute drive?"

As she hauled their suitcases onto a cart, a slightly built figure came running towards them.

"Leela aunty! Meena aunty!"

The young woman waved at them. From the down coat to the woollen cap she had clamped down on her head, she was perfectly clad to ward off the icy cold of Vermont's winter.

"My apologies for not getting here earlier — the traffic on Route 7 was horrendous!"

They haven't changed one bit, she thought. As she walked towards them, she saw a short, very plump woman with tortoiseshell glasses, her iron-grey hair pulled back into a severe bun — her Leela aunty. Her liquid brown eyes, retroussé nose, and pointy ears had always reminded Madhu and her friend, Murali, of an inquisitive plump wren. She was composed entirely of bulges. The other woman — her Meena aunty — couldn't have presented a greater contrast. Meena Rao was thin to the point of being scrawny. Her oval face was framed by very short silver-grey hair with a natural wave in it. She was unusually tall for a South-Asian woman. Her thick salt-and-pepper eyebrows jutted out like a cliff overhang, shielding small shrewd eyes above a distinctly aquiline nose. Had she been a bird-watcher, Madhu would have compared Meena to a great blue heron. Her greenish-blue eyes were a surprising feature, a colour rare in a person of South-Asian origin. Leela Rao certainly exuded what Madhu would have termed grandmotherliness, an attribute that hardly bespoke the keen analytic mind of a Sherlock Holmes or a Jane Marple, although her sharp eyes said otherwise. Meena's bony frame did not encourage cuddling.

Leela forgot her frustration at the sight of the charming smile that accompanied Madhu's apologies.

"Not a problem, child."

Meena added, "Your timing is great. We just got our luggage."

The cousins hugged the slight, yet muscular figure of the woman whose mother, Komal, had been a cherished friend. Madhu cautioned, "Put on your coats and gloves. It's freezing outside."

Madhu pushed the cart to her car. As they drove off in the Mini Cooper Coupe, Madhu said, "It'll take us about forty minutes to get back to my apartment. Would you like some real food before we set out?"

Leela let out a sigh of relief.

"You're a mind reader, Madhu! You haven't forgotten, have you, that your Leela aunty has never said 'no' to refreshment of any kind? And after almost seven hours of cramped seating, peanuts or mini pretzels, and watery coffee, I am ready for some 'real' food as you call it!"

"Me too!" Meena echoed.

They smiled. Madhu asked, "How about some good seafood?"

She got two vigorous nods and they headed for Bleu Northeast Seafood on Cherry Street. An hour later, they sat back sipping cappuccinos and absorbing the view of the Green Mountains. Leela burped softly and contentedly, and began, "So, tell us, Madhu dear! The homicides. From what I have read, this Sean O'Flaherty was certainly Hall of Fame material. What reason would someone have to kill him?"

"I can name a dozen! Professional jealousy for one. He thought he was god's gift to sports and women. Could have been an abused girlfriend. He was a coward, and cowardice is typically the other side of the bully coin. Talk about narcissism! Sean O'Flaherty was very much in love with Sean O'Flaherty."

"Any leads?"

"Well, I've been sworn to secrecy since I saw O'Flaherty's body…"

The cousins stared at Madhu.

"What?" Meena cried out. "You discovered the athlete?"

"Yes. And it was not only decapitated, but someone had carved Arabic calligraphy spelling out 'Al-ḥamdu lillāh'."

The cousins cried out in unison:

"That's dreadful! That's barbaric!"

"The police don't want what smacks of ritualistic killing to be made public — with all this hatred of Islam where an entire religion is so easily equated with terrorism, it could quickly escalate to mass hysteria."

Her cell phone buzzed. She listened intently for a few seconds.

"Yes, Sergeant Erickson, I'll come over as soon as I can. I'm in Burlington, just picked up friends of mine from the airport. It'll take about forty minutes for us to get back."

Madhu pocketed her cell, a troubled look on her face. She said, "Chief Inspector Bonnie Martel, who's in charge of the investigation, has requested me to come to the station to clarify a few things. Would the two of you do me a huge favor? Come along with me? Hold my hand?"

The cousins nodded vigorously.

"Wild horses couldn't drag us away!" Leela said, thumping the table with her fist.

March 18: Beethoven's love letter

The cousins and Madhu got to the station just as Sergeant Erickson came through the intricately carved wooden front door of Montpelier City Hall. Erickson led Madhu to Chief Bonnie Martel's office, with Leela and Meena following at a discreet distance.

"Ladies," the sergeant politely waved the cousins to a wooden bench against the wall. "Please wait here."

Police Chief Bonnie Martel got up as Madhu entered her office.

"Professor Trivedi! Take a seat, please! Thank you for obliging us so quickly."

Madhu was stunned. She hadn't expected such a genial reception from the police. One more stereotype down the tube! The chief looked intently at Madhu.

"There's something that might shed more light on O'Flaherty's death. We found this in your mailbox."

She pushed a letter and several photographs towards Madhu. A gasp escaped her when she saw the first photo.

"What the... This is outrageous!"

The photo showed her with Sean O'Flaherty in what could only be described as a compromising position. O'Flaherty was kneeling and Madhu appeared to be hugging him tightly. The three remaining images were equally explicit. She unfolded the letter and read:

Though still in bed, my thoughts go out to you, my Immortal Beloved, now and then joyfully, then sadly, waiting to learn whether or not fate will hear us... I will never give you up, my Beloved. Yours forever!

She burst out laughing.

"You find this amusing, Professor Trivedi?"

"No, Chief Inspector, no! I'm not barmy! You must think me... It's just that... I should explain! Some weeks ago, I discussed how music could be a religious experience. As an example, I played Beethoven's Fifth and one of Thyaagaraaja's Kritis in the rāgam Hindōḷam.[8] We read several love letters written by musicians to their various muses. One of them was supposedly written by Beethoven to his lover."

She looked at Bonnie Martel.

"Lover boy here has copied Beethoven's letter word for word, except for the 'give you up' part. It is... Was so typical of Sean. To plagiarize, I mean."

Her eyes fell again on the photos.

---

[8] Thyaagaraaja (May 4, 1767 — January 6, 1847) was one of the greatest composers of Carnatic music or South Indian classical music. Hindōḷam is a rāgam (musical scale of South Indian classical music) in Carnatic music. Kriti or krti is the format of a musical composition typical to Carnatic music. It forms the backbone of any Carnatic music concert and is the longer format of a song. (Source: Wikipedia)

"I don't understand! Where... How... I cannot for the life of me..."

She suddenly stopped.

"Damn!"

"Yes, Professor? Something you want to tell me?"

"Yes! It was a week or so ago. Sean rushed into my room and threw himself at my feet, burying his face in my lap. I tried to push him away, but he held me in this really tight grip. He was pleading for a better grade. I finally threatened him with security."

A look of horror spread across her face.

"An accomplice?"

Chief Inspector Martel said, "More likely a hidden camera. A tiny digital cam would have done the trick. He could have placed it in your room beforehand. Do you leave your office unlocked?"

"Yes, of course, during the day. I'm in and out all the time. Only when I leave for the day do I remember to lock it. There have been a couple of thefts — computers mainly."

"So, anybody knowing your routine, your class schedule, could have walked into your office."

"I suppose," Madhu replied. "Well..."

"The letter may have been a prelude to blackmailing you perhaps," the Chief said. "But we have to figure out who would have a motive to kill Sean."

"I can't think of anybody who would want to kill him." She grinned wryly. "Me, yes. Sean hated me for the bad grades I kept dishing out. And Coach Miller was mad as hell with me. He paid me a rather abrupt visit recently, trying to convince me to give Sean better grades. When I refused, he was furious, went behind my back to the Dean of Students."

"And how did the Dean react?"

"Well, he sent me this preachy email in which he practically accused me of arbitrarily handing out bad grades."

"Interesting!" The chief leaned back in her chair. "It seems that the ivory tower is not immune to primal emotions! What about your other students?"

"I have had my share of disgruntled students, of course. And I've harbored murderous thoughts towards many a lazy kid in my classes. But murdering Sean — I can't help you there. It could have been professional jealousy, a girlfriend scorned or abused. He was a coward and a bully. I was telling my guests just now that Sean O'Flaherty was very much in love with Sean O'Flaherty."

The chief inspector nodded, made notes on her iPad, and said, "Something else, Professor. You may not have heard yet, but there has been another homicide. You might be able to shed some light on it."

"Another murder! Who was it? And you say I…"

"Your student, Martin McDonald…"

"No!" Madhu cried out. "Please! Not Martin! Oh my god, what is happening?"

"No, Professor Trivedi, no! I'm sorry, I should have begun this differently. It was Martin's friend, Ignatius Munyaradzi, an exchange student from Zimbabwe."

"That's ghastly! Poor Martin! I visited them once in their studio apartment. They were very much in love."

"What can you tell me about Ignatius?"

"Only that he was the first in his family to leave his home in Harare. How…"

"The same MO — blunt force trauma, then decapitation. No murder weapon on the scene. And the same Arabic calligraphy on the chest. I'm waiting to hear back from Forensics about any other evidence at both crime scenes."

She extended her hand to Madhu.

"Thank you, Professor Trivedi! This killer may be targeting certain types of students. If you think of anything connecting the two murders, please call me at once. And please be careful!"

Madhu smiled forlornly.

"I believe I have that covered, Chief. I just picked up two very dear friends — two seventy-six-year-old South-Asian women from Tucson. They are also the local superwomen, having helped solve several serial killings. And they have this incredible talent for discovering surprising connections."

She missed the thoughtful look on the chief's face as she left the room.

March 19: Leela and Meena threaten to investigate

Madhu sat in her living room facing the cousins.

"You look exhausted, child!" Leela said. "Here!" She pointed to a plate of chocolate chip cookies. "I like the way you stock your cupboards with snacks — and nothing wimpy about them either! And drink some of the tea we prepared."

Madhu sighed.

"It's been a tough couple of days. Two homicides, both linked to the college. And Ignatius' murder is especially tragic. His parents are expected here tomorrow to take his body back to Harare, that is as soon as the ME has finished his examination."

"What does your Chief Inspector say?"

"They're looking for something to link the two killings. Since the MO is similar, they're thinking a single killer."

Leela said, "Have they found the murder weapon or weapons?"

"No, not yet."

"Do you think she'd mind if we did a little 'investigation' of our own?"

Madhu sighed again. Leela smiled.

"We would talk. You know we have a talent for talking!"

"Don't I know it!" Madhu grinned. "So, where do you want to begin?"

"For starters, we ought to talk to the people who have links with the boys, however tenuous. Martin, his parents, Ignatius' parents, the O'Flahertys, the coach, the Dean of Students. A second tier would be O'Flaherty's teammates and... Did you say Ignatius worked as a TA in the African Studies Department? Well, we'll have to talk to students and faculty in that department. That's just for starters. It would be best if Chief Martel didn't know about our involvement! We wouldn't want her to feel threatened — it's a matter of turf."

Madhu affectionately slapped Leela's hand.

"I'd forgotten your Machiavellian mind, Leela aunty!"

She felt her smartphone vibrate.

"Oh! Hi, Chief Martel! What can I...? Yes, they are here with me. Just a second."

She looked at the cousins.

"For you, gals! Chief Inspector Bonnie Martel herself!"

She smiled.

"Even if I wanted to, I couldn't stop you, could I? What devious plans do you have?"

Leela took the phone, switched on the speaker, and spoke briefly.

"Yes, Chief Inspector, of course. We'd be glad to assist any way we can. Now? Let me check with Madhu — Professor Trivedi."

She looked at Madhu who nodded.

"Yes, Chief Inspector, she can drive us over right away."

Five minutes later, the cousins and Madhu faced Martel in the City Hall.

"This is rather unorthodox, Professor Leela Rao, Ms Meena Rao, but when I heard from Professor Trivedi that you had helped solve several crimes, I just couldn't resist calling on you for help. And Bureau Chief Murali Kalluri from Tucson had the highest praise for your sleuthing instincts!"

"You checked our credentials!" Leela said, glancing complacently at her cousin. "Well, well! Tell us, chief, what have you got so far?"

"We're at a dead end as of now. What we have…" Martel said, checking her notes. "… Are two murders with seemingly similar MOs. The ME believes death was due to blunt force trauma in both cases. I just got a report from my sergeant that they came across a trophy stolen from the Department of Cultural Studies in the garbage dump near the apartment building of the second victim. DNA analysis of blood and hair on the head of the trophy belonged to the two victims. And both were decapitated post mortem. And there is that Arabic calligraphy carved into the chest, also post mortem. We have means and opportunity. But where the heck is the motive?"

She looked at Leela.

"One other thing. The ME who studied Sean O'Flaherty's body found clear evidence of alcoholism — the liver was pretty shot for someone so young. I sent officers to the O'Flaherty home to search his room. They found several empty bottles of gin and vodka. We checked his emails and smartphone but came up empty. If he was at all involved in something illegal, he either covered his tracks extremely well or…"

"Or someone erased everything?" Leela finished the chief's thought. "What about Ignatius?"

"Ah yes, Ignatius. Well, stomach contents showed that he had had pizza an hour before his death. No trace elements of poisons or toxins were found."

She ran her fingers through her short auburn hair, frustration in every stroke.

"Professor Rao, both sets of parents are anxiously waiting to bury their sons. I am being pressured by the mayor to come up soon with arrests. Bureau Chief Kalluri told us that you have done a lot of research into ritual killings."

Leela nodded. Chief Martel continued, "I would like both of you to look at the bodies; tell us what you see."

They drove to the facility where the Chief Medical Officer had performed the autopsies.

March 20: Parents grieve

The Munyaradzis stood dazedly at the baggage claim
area. Mrs Munyaradzi wiped her eyes repeatedly with a
shawl. A consular officer from the US embassy,
accompanied by an official from the Mugabe
government, had escorted them to Harare International
Airport and cleared them quickly through customs and
immigration. President Carlos Juarez had contacted
Vermont's Lieutenant Governor for help in getting the
Munyaradzis as quickly as possible to the U.S. The
Mugabe government, suitably impressed by a request
from a senior government official, waived the usual
bureaucratic red-tape. However, the Zimbabwean
official who hugged Mr Munyaradzi at the airport, in an
apparent show of shared grief, felt an envelope of cash
being slipped into his coat pocket. It was business as
usual.

The couple waited with ever-increasing anxiety,
and Mr Munyaradzi repeatedly looked at his
smartphone for messages. A moment later, a tall
policeman strode towards them.

"This is a bad sign. A policeman coming towards
us — what shall we do, husband?" Mrs Munyaradzi
whispered, dabbing her brow with a white lace

handkerchief. "Twenty hours of torture in those planes, and now this?"

"Mr and Mrs Munyaradzi? I am Sergeant Erickson, here to take you to Anderson College. May I help you with your luggage?"

***

President Carlos Juarez took a deep breath. Since Sean O'Flaherty's murder, there had been a worrisome withdrawal of students from the college. Parents and guardians were panicking. And now a second murder — violence doesn't beget trust. He entered the packed auditorium. He had instructed the provost to invite community members to attend. They filled more than half the space. Juarez took a deep breath. The next few minutes might make or break the college.

"Anderson College students, faculty, and staff — and members of our community! I address you once again with sad news indeed. A second life has been lost to us, again in a violent manner, the life of Ignatius Munyaradzi, a life that his parents had entrusted to us for safekeeping."

Juarez took a deep breath and continued, "Town and gown — we have to work together; we need each other as never before. Together, we will be able to find and punish those monsters who have threatened the fabric of our society. Together, we will once again be able to guarantee the safety of our entire community."

He beckoned to Chief Inspector Bonnie Martel to join him on the podium.

"Many of you are familiar with our Chief. Chief Inspector Martel, would you brief us?"

Bonnie Martel took the mike from Juarez's hands.

"Thank you, President Juarez. We have several leads. I am very confident that we will be able to find the killer or killers. I have also commissioned some of my officers to assist campus security. President Juarez and I have also initiated several safety measures."

A voice made itself heard from the audience.

"President Juarez and Chief Inspector Martel, don't you think it is advisable to shut down the college until the safety of our children is assured?"

The president said, "Chief, would you be so good?"

Bonnie Martel looked at the elderly woman who had spoken.

"Rosie, thank you for being here! I don't know how the post office is functioning without you!"

Rosie Cameron smiled. There was relieved laughter in the hall.

Martel continued, "I appreciate your concern and your advice. But closing down the college is tantamount to surrendering to the killers. We cannot allow them to think that we can be so easily terrorized. Let me list the measures we have already taken:

1. Set up crisis centres and hotlines at the college's Counselling and Testing Center;

2. Installed closed-circuit television in all residence and lecture halls, as well as in the corridors;

3. Installed metal detectors at the entrances to the libraries, dining halls, and gyms;

4. Posted safety measures on every door in our residence halls advising residents not to prop doors open, to report any suspicious activity, to stay in well-lit, well-travelled areas if they are walking outside, and to call our emergency hotline (802-433-HELP);

5. Told students not to go anywhere alone.

This hotline number has been posted everywhere, especially in closed spaces like lavatories and bathing areas."

She looked around for more questions or concerns. President Juarez spoke into the mike, "I give you my solemn promise that we will do everything to punish these monsters who can destroy human life so callously."

"Honourable Mr President, sir," a voice made itself heard from the back of the auditorium. "My wife and I wish to express our gratitude for your sincere efforts to track down the evil spirit who took away our son."

The auditorium turned as one to look at the owner of the voice. A tall man dressed in the traditional Zimbabwean outfit of headdress and wraparound cloth bowed to the gathering. His wife, also traditionally robed, joined him in bowing. President Juarez and Chief Inspector Martel stepped down from the podium and walked towards the couple.

March 21: Sarducci's

Madhu looked at her bed. Piles of dresses and saris covered it. Had she regressed? She giggled. She hadn't felt this lightheaded since that crush she had had in high school on that gorgeous hockey player. What a hunk! And his dark brown eyes — bedroom eyes. She giggled again. Stop it! You are a mature woman. It's just one evening! Charles is stunning. He had called her twice since that evening at the Stowe Mountain Lodge. Before he could call again and turn this into a 'hard to get' pattern — something she strenuously wished to avoid — she had asked him to visit her on campus. That first meeting had been followed by a few informal rendezvous in *The Thirsty Thistle*, the college cafeteria. And then it had come, an invite to dinner.

She finally decided on a deep purple silk caftan that a friend from Kenya had brought her. Matching earrings and bangles, discreet make-up, a dab of perfume, and she was ready for him. When the doorbell rang, she inhaled deeply, and gratuitously patted her hair that she had fashioned into a Dutch braid. She wasn't prepared for what greeted her eyes as she opened the door. Charles was wearing traditional Zimbabwean headdress and wraparound cloth. The canary yellow of the cloth brilliantly contrasted with her own purple caftan. He bowed, offered his arm, and led her out to his purple Maserati, a coupé after her own heart.

"No," he said laughing. "I didn't plan to colour code anything! Honestly, purple is one of my favourite colors," he added. "I had it custom-painted when I bought it last year. And I hope you like Italian food. Since I invited you, I hoped you wouldn't mind my choosing the restaurant. But as my guest, do let me know if you'd rather go elsewhere."

"Sarducci's is fine with me, Charles."

She couldn't tear her eyes away from the seductive curves of the car.

"Oh! A gift from the company. The profits were especially good last year."

She had almost forgotten that he was a top executive. This was a clear reminder that he was in a different league when it came to money. But that wouldn't prevent her from enjoying the moment. She leaned back into the soft leather. It promised to be a memorable evening.

Madhu loved the space that the restaurant occupied. The maître d' seated them inside because of the wintry weather, but they could look out at the Winooski River. The building had been an old grain warehouse. But with inspired ideas from some of Montpelier's best architects, the interior's detail work had managed to create an invitingly elegant ambience.

"Would you like to order the wine?" Charles asked.

This was a man in a million, she thought. She looked at the reds and suggested a 2012 Montepulciano d'Abruzzo.

"I think I'll like it," he said. "I've never had it."

"Neither have I!" she grinned. "The name just sounds so… So…"

"Italian?" he grinned back.

She tasted the wine that the maître d', surprised at the gender reversal, offered her. It had a hint of mocha and reminded her of ripe cherries and plums She nodded enthusiastically. The next hour passed by in a blur of bruschetta al pomodoro, succulent wood roasted Salmon, and apple and hazelnut salad. They leaned back over orders of crème caramel for her and gelato for him. Their waiter had just placed two frothy cups of cappuccinos on the table.

"May I ask you an indiscreet question?"

"You may," she said, her mind completely relaxed for the first time in days.

"How is it that such a beautiful, intelligent woman is still single?"

"I've had my taste of connubial 'bliss' — it is highly overrated. And to return the compliment — what about you? You are beautiful and intelligent."

"Touché! My parents tried to arrange several marriages for me from the Shona. But growing up in the UK showed me other possibilities. But none of those worked out for me — unfortunately."

"The Shona — that's the same ethnic group to which Ignatius belonged!"

"Yes. Talking about Ignatius, have the police come up with any leads about the killers?"

"None as far as I know. They're keeping a tight lid on both the murders."

"The students must be traumatized."

"Yes. We have brought in grief counsellors. Charles, it just occurred to me — you may have met Ignatius. He mentioned that a few Zimbabweans from Chicago had recently met in Montpelier to discuss the possibility of creating a Zimbabwe Association similar to that in the UK. You could have met him there!"

"I did go to that meeting. But I don't remember Ignatius. It was quite a big gathering. The organizers invited members of various cultural and charitable organizations. I was invited to discuss their application for a donation from McMoran. The intent was to create a foundation for offering internships to young Zimbabweans, especially the children of those migrants who are understandably conflicted about returning to Zimbabwe. Hyperinflation, the black market, Mugabe's one-party tyranny… The list goes on and on."

He looked intently at Madhu.

"You think he might have been targeted for attending that meeting? But why? And by whom? Is that what the cops are assuming?"

"I don't know," she burst out. "And really — I'm not in the confidence of the police!"

"Sorry! Didn't mean to imply anything like that. I just meant… Since you have been privy to all those harrowingly gruesome ritualistic details since discovering that athlete's body…"

Madhu immediately regretted her outburst.

"Let's change the topic, shall we? I've been getting an earful from my guests."

"Your aunts, right?"

"Well, I call them 'aunts' — we South-Asians have this habit of calling older acquaintances and friends 'uncles' and 'aunties'!"

"That's really touching! And you say they travelled quite a distance to be with you?"

"Did I? Well, that is true. They live in Tucson, Arizona. Both retired, both adventurous spirits like you won't believe! They have solved at least six serial and other killings in the last six years."

"Fascinating!" Charles beckoned to the waiter.

"Another bottle of the same, Madhu? Or would you like to try something different?"

"Nothing more for me, Charles! I need to keep a clear head for tomorrow. My review committee member will be in the classroom."

"Then I will refrain too! I just realized it's good to keep a clear head when I'm with you."

He signalled to the waiter for the check.

May 22: The cousins go a-hunting

"Shall we…" Leela said.

"…Make a list of people we want to talk to, then divvy them up, right?" Meena finished.

"Stop, fathead! Stop finishing my sentences! We have become that thing I have always dreaded — an old married couple!"

"That's good! I can imagine our dearly departed hubbies looking at us from wherever they are and laughing their heads off. Okay, here goes," Meena said opening her laptop. "You take on the students. And I'll tackle faculty and staff."

Leela entered Martin Luther King Hall and took the elevator up to the Department of Cultural Studies. Department Head Christopher Reay had given her permission to meet those students who wished to talk about Sean O'Flaherty. Interdepartmental administrative assistant Lucy Gilmore led her to an empty office.

"Professor Rao, we have reserved this room for you. The students have been instructed to come in one by one."

"Excellent. Thank you, Ms Gilmore."

Leela took out a pad and pencil. Meena's attempts to introduce her to an iPad had failed miserably.

"May I come in, Professor?"

The door opened a crack and an anxious face framed by a mop of untidy black curls peeped in.

"Come in! You are?"

"Sheila, Sheila Gilmore. My mother — Lucy Gilmore — works for the department head here. Mother told me you, like, wanted to ask us about Sean. Are you really Professor Trivedi's professor?"

Leela smiled.

"I was her teacher."

"Wow! I like the prof; I like her a lot. She's a great teacher, you know. Professor Rao, I... I don't have much time. My next class begins in fifteen minutes. But I would really like to talk about Ignatius."

"You knew him?"

"Well, Marty... Martin and I are close. And Iggy was, like, Martin's boyfriend. We hung out."

"What about Sean O'Flaherty?"

"He's... He was a real jerk — thought he was all that."

She saw Leela's puzzled expression.

"I mean, he thought he was superior."

She grinned suddenly.

"He was like, I mean, like so super ticked off that I didn't want to go out with him. And he baited Marty all the time! Harassed him! Made, like, racial and antigay slurs when he saw Iggy. Called him all kinds of antigay shit like 'Freak' and 'F*g' and 'Homo'."

"How did Martin and Ignatius react to these taunts? Did they strike back?"

"No, no!" Sheila looked shocked. "They wouldn't. They're, like, pacifists, you know — people who don't believe in violence."

"I understand," Leela said. "Anything else you noticed that you'd like to share?"

"Well, there was, like, one time, this weird thing last week. The three of us were going to the movies. But this guy comes up to Iggy, from like nowhere. Iggy tells Marty and me to go ahead — he'll catch up. But he didn't, he didn't catch the movie. He was waiting for us outside — he looked awful. We tried to, like, find out what happened, who that guy was. But he, like, just clammed up!"

"Do you remember what this man looked like?"

"Tall. He had on this real long black winter coat. I couldn't really make out much. All of him was, like, muffled up. Sorry!"

She looked at her watch and exclaimed, "Excuse me, Professor, have to rush. But I could come back."

Leela shook her head.

"Thank you, but not at the moment. You've been very helpful. And I'm so sorry for the loss of your friend."

"Yeah — he was really cool."

There were tears in her eyes as she left the room. Half a dozen interviews later, Leela left the room to get some coke from the machine in the corridor. Not one of them had anything bad to say about O'Flaherty. Sheila was the only one to bring new information to light. Leela looked at the list of names in front of her. A knock on the door and a tall blond student entered. He looked surprised to see Leela. She knew that look which said: "You belong in one of those third-world countries or an old people's assisted living!" She knew exactly how to deal with such an attitude. She lowered her voice to the deep foghorn timbre that never failed to intimidate students. Her imitation of old army generals never failed to get a laugh out of family and friends.

"Sit! Name?"

"Chuck… Charles Swinburne, Professor."

It was almost comical to see how quickly Chuck Swinburne responded. His face reddened as he sat down gingerly on a chair.

"He was Alpha Greek," he explained, remembering where he was. "I mean, he was great."

He slowed down, carefully choosing his words.

"He was a great quarterback."

"What about in class? How was he academically?"

"Academically? Oh, I suppose he was good in 'demics… Academics."

Leela looked at him thoughtfully. He studiously avoided her eyes. *He's hiding something. That twitching — I've seen that too often. He's shooting up.*

"Something you want to tell me, Swinburne?"

"My parents say one shouldn't say anything bad about the dead. But…"

"But what, Swinburne?"

"Sean was dealing. Now that he's dead, I suppose it can, like, come out, can't it?"

He looked appealingly at Leela.

"Drugs?" she asked, leaning forward and willing him to talk.

"Yes, ma'am."

He took a bottle of water out of his backpack and emptied it in one big gulp.

"Now, Swinburne, tell me in your own words what you know about Sean O'Flaherty."

Thirst — dry mouth. Meth?

"How about you, Swinburne? Do you indulge?"

"You mean, do I… No, no, absolutely not, nada."

"Tell me the truth if you don't want to be an accessory after the fact."

"But sir… Ma'am! I don't shoot up!"

"What are you hiding, Swinburne?"

Droplets of sweat began gathering on his forehead.

"I just meant — when I said Sean dealt — I went to a couple of parties he gave."

He suddenly lost his nervousness.

"Man, they rocked!"

Leela cracked down the whip again.

"Explain!"

"I mean, it was like in Hollywood — lots of booze, hot chicks, high-class food like caviar and stuff."

"He was rich?"

"Yes, like, crazy rich, man! One time, one time he used hundred-dollar bills to…"

He bit his tongue.

"To snort?" Leela finished. He kept quiet.

"Dismissed, Swinburne!"

He jumped up and ran out of the room.

A little later, an exhausted Leela sat in Madhu's living room sipping strong sweet milky tea laced with ginger and other spices. She picked up the last of a batch of freshly baked cookies and plopped it into her mouth with relish.

"So, tell me, Leela aunty, how did it go?"

"Clearly, O'Flaherty was making money from dealing. But by the sound of it, he was spending it in a spectacular fashion. Dad and Mom away in Harare, nobody to supervise him."

Leela stood up.

"I've got to get back to campus. Have two more kids who've signed up to talk."

As she entered the elevator to the ride up to the Department of Cultural Studies, a heavy-set swarthy student cried out: "Hold it!"

He rushed in and thanked her. They exited on the same floor. The student ran awkwardly out of the elevator and walked as quickly as his weight permitted to Christopher Reay's office, and stood outside panting.

As Leela opened the door, the student's eyes widened with surprise.

"Professor Rao? I'm so sorry! I should have known. My name is Abdelkarim al-Adel."

"Come on in, Mr al-Adel! Take a seat!"

She saw before him a young man about six feet in height. He sat down and breathed heavily. Puppy fat! Parents indulge him. Could be an only child. His olive complexion, dark brown eyes, and short curly black hair placed him somewhere in the Middle East. Egypt, she told herself. A fellow anthropologist at the University of Cairo had the same name. She studied him for a couple of minutes, turning over in her mind several approaches to the conversation.

"Mr al-Adel, why Anderson?"

"Beg your pardon?"

"Why did you choose Anderson College for your undergrad studies?"

"I see. Well, madame, my father is Egypt's Deputy Chief of Mission to the US. He wants me to follow in his footsteps. During his term in this country — he predicts that he'll be here for at least seven years — he wants me to get my undergrad degree in international affairs."

"Why not choose the School of International Service in D.C.? Theirs is one of the top programs in the country. And of course, your parents are right there."

al-Adel grinned sheepishly. "Well, Egyptian parents can be…"

"Rather over-protective? If they are anything like Indian parents, I can imagine it very well! You are a sophomore, correct?"

"Yes, madame."

"How do you like it so far?"

"It was difficult at first. But it's getting better."

"Have you made friends?"

"Yes. A couple. You have been asking about Sean O'Flaherty? Well, I would like to add something about him."

"Go ahead."

"Sean was the one who made life very difficult for me, along with his buddies."

"Like Charles Swinburne?"

The sophomore looked surprised.

"Yes, Madame, like Swinburne. They... They disrespected me and my faith, especially O'Flaherty. They would post hate mail on my dorm door. And they posted a photograph on Facebook showing a man photoshopped to look like me in bed with a woman in a niqab. And the caption below ran: 'How the prophet Muhammed rewards his followers.' When I challenged O'Flaherty the next day, he laughed — called me a headbanger."

"A reference to the way you bow your head, during prayers?"

"Yes. Also 'Osama' and 'Rag-head' and 'Terr-ab.'"

"I see — 'Terrorist-Arab.'"

"O'Flaherty was the worst, madame. He hounded me day and night. One time — he must have been high — he burst into my room dressed up to look like our prophet, *alayhi as- salām*,[9] and… Madame, I am so ashamed — it is an obscenity… And exposed himself."

He hid his face in his hands. He had reached breaking point. Leela got up and laid a gentle hand on his shoulder.

"Son, thank you for your honesty. And remember, he cannot hurt you any more."

al-Adel had a strange expression on his face.

"No, he cannot."

He got up, salaamed Leela, and left. For several minutes, Leela stared unseeingly at the door. There was so much rage in the O'Flaherty killing.

---

[9] Peace be upon him.

May 22: A hoodie is caved in

Carleton Murray opened his eyes even before the alarm had a chance to wake him up. It was three forty-five in the morning. He smiled broadly as he began planning his day on his farm in Cabot, VT. He and his wife had left their high-powered executive jobs in New York City six years before to look after the farm his father had bequeathed to him. As a child, he had loved the soil, the dung, and the smell of the farm animals. The first time his dad had allowed him to milk a cow, he hadn't been able to sleep a wink. It was time to look after his Jersey cows. Molly hadn't been feeding too well. He'd have to check with the large animal vet Larry Massie about her.

This morning was special. He had been feeding his cows special grain and organic hay to produce more savoury milk. And now he had launched into the exciting new field — or very ancient field, depending on which way one looked at it — of making cave-aged cheese. Both he and his wife believed staunchly in sustainable farming. Using stones from the hills in Panton, they had built a cave on the farm to replicate, as closely as possible, the aging process used for centuries, before refrigeration. Today was the day to turn and brush the ten-pound wheel of cheese in order to create a natural rind. He looked at his sleeping wife. Let her sleep a little while longer. She had had a rough night with their eight-month-old.

Carleton put on his sheepskin coat and fur-lined boots. May mornings in Cabot were just a tad above freezing. He pulled on his leather gloves and headed for the cave. He opened the reinforced steel door to the 'cave' and pushed aside the heavy burlap curtain behind it. Then he stood still and sniffed expectantly. The aroma of ripening cheese — he couldn't wait to taste this new batch. But it took patience. He flicked the light switch on and gazed at the two rows of ten-pound wheels. He took out a brush and was about to treat the first wheel when his foot stumbled against something soft.

"This is 911. What is your emergency?"

***

The two cops looked at the body of the dead man. He was wearing a hoodie.

"This was execution-style," the first one said.

"Yup! Just like in 'The Untouchables,' the other said, his voice filled with awe. "I'm pretty sure the chief hasn't seen anything like this!"

"Well, we might have to call in the FBI! Wow! Just imagine the feds coming here to our town!"

Carleton Murray cleared his throat.

"Officers, the paramedics are here. What will happen to him?"

"This is a homicide; he'll be taken to the Office of the Chief Medical Examiner in Burlington."

The other uniform added, "Mr Murray, we'll contact you for further questioning."

Murray looked at wife Marie, then back at the cop.

"If word gets out that they found a dead body in our cheese cave, our business will plunge, possibly disappear. Is there any way this can be kept quiet?"

"It is not for us to say, sir. The chief will get in touch with you regarding the matter. Good day sir, ma'am!"

Two hours later, the Chief Medical Examiner looked at the body on the autopsy table. He dictated his report into a recorder.

"Date and hour autopsy performed: 5/22/2006; five thirty p.m. by Dr Michael Borden, M.D., 303 Cherry Avenue, Burlington, VT. Assistant: Sherry Whiner, M.D. Full autopsy performed. Name: John Doe. Date of Birth: unknown. Race: White. Sex: Male. Date of Death: between 5/17 and 5/18/2006. Coroner's Case #: 2006-488. Investigative Agency: Chittenden County, Office of the Chief Medical Examiner. External examination: The autopsy began at five thirty p.m. on May 22, 2006. The body was presented in a black body bag. The victim was wearing blue jeans, a white cotton vest, and a black hoodie."

The report confirmed that the man had been directly shot into the top of his head, a wound that was "not survivable."

May 22: Meena Rao probes further

Dean of Students Hugh McCormick finished signing some letters. He leaned back and looked at the wall in front of him, covered with all the degrees, awards, and distinctions he had received in forty years of teaching and administration. He took off his reading glasses and rubbed his tired eyes. He badly wanted to retire. Students' sense of entitlement had increased exponentially in the last decade. These private colleges were all the same. The old boys network governed how the kids were educated. It didn't matter how they performed in the courses. In the end, their transcripts were carefully 'edited', and daddy's little boy or girl carried on the billion-dollar family business. Any ideals he might have had once had vanished. And other avenues for making a quick buck had opened up rapidly.

McCormick opened the desk drawer and rolled himself a joint. Ah! Never lets me down. With every new batch of faculty, he was finding it increasingly difficult to persuade them to bend the rules. Not that they were less corruptible, but he was getting tired of having to woo them. He had enough in his Caymans account. He thought back to the last forty years. Flexibility had been the name of the game, especially when contracts with managers of the major leagues had to be negotiated. And a few past presidents had proven less principled than the present incumbent, which was all he had needed to feather his nest.

When he had joined Anderson some forty-five years ago, he had been as naively idealistic as some of the kids here. He had sworn to uphold the college's mission of maintaining the highest of academic standards amongst its athletes. He had himself been a star athlete at his alma mater, the University of Connecticut. But competition had become fierce in recent years. And two failed marriages and ruinous child support payments had rapidly eroded those ideals. Sean O'Flaherty had been a most promising athlete. Several scouts had looked at him carefully, had discussed future prospects with Coach Miller. But the coach was getting greedier, demanding more than a fifty-fifty split. And this new wrinkle — Sean's murder — was bad for business. He'd have to get out soon.

The dean's administrative assistant knocked on the door. "Your next appointment is here, Hugh. A Ms Meena Rao."

"Thank you, Alice. Give me a minute, will you?"

He hurriedly snuffed the joint, took out a can of deodorizer, and sprayed the stuff into the air around him. He glanced at a mirror below his college degree and adjusted his hair and tie. He had accumulated quite a bit of flab around the midriff and paid his tailor obscene amounts of money to tailor his suits in an appropriately flattering manner.

Satisfied that the air was clean, he went to the door and let in a tall, gaunt woman with very short salt-and-pepper hair. She was dressed in a fashionable dark blue suit. A single string of freshwater pearls was the only jewelry she wore.

"Dean McCormick? Thank you for seeing me." She shook the offered hand.

"Please, take a seat, Ms Rao. I'm sorry your visit with my colleague Madhu Trivedi isn't under more favorable circumstances."

Since her retirement from her job as a high-powered corporate lawyer in New York City, Meena had stuffed every single tailor-made suit she possessed into a large chest, poured a bag of mothballs into it, and hauled it into the garage. She surreptitiously sniffed her sleeve as she sat down. The smell of mothballs wasn't that strong any more. She had aired the suit for several days now, had even sprayed it with Eau de Cologne. She had packed the suit as an afterthought, for emergencies. And this certainly counted as one. All she smelt here was an intense odour of... What was it? Lysol? Leela always cursed her for having such an acute sense of smell. Something else. Ugh! Sickly sweet.

"You're right, Dean McCormick, circumstances could have been more favourable. But the fact of the matter is, Madhu sent us an urgent request to be with her. She is really stressed out about the murders."

She added, carefully watching the man's face, "My cousin, Professor Leela Rao…"

"Yes, our honoured keynote speaker."

"Yes. She and I have helped solve some murders in the past. We might be of help here, too."

The Trivedi woman actually asked this person to come here because of the murders? What is she up to? The Dean composed his features and got up in a gesture of dismissal. He didn't need any meddling old amateur sleuths here.

"That is very good of you, Ms Rao, but I believe Chief Inspector Martel has everything under control. Anything else I can help you with?"

She had obviously struck a nerve. It would be prudent not to continue the conversation. She had achieved her objective — she had rattled him! Now she had to find out why.

"No, thank you. I had no intention of interfering. My apologies. And thank you for your time."

She got up and left the room without shaking his hand again. Worry lines remained etched on the man's forehead — she noted them with satisfaction.

***

Coach Jeb Miller came out of the men's locker room. He was not happy, not happy at all. His contact had just blown him off, had told him profits were slipping. He needed to finalize the next shipment soon. Well, he would have to... What the heck? A tall woman with very short salt-and-pepper hair had just bumped into him.

"Oh, excuse me! I'm looking for Coach Miller, Coach Jeb Miller?"

Miller looked at her. Smartly dressed, too thin for his taste. Wonder what the woman wants.

"That's me! How can I help you, lady?"

"Coach Miller, my name is Meena Rao. I'm here with my cousin, Professor Leela Rao, the college's keynote speaker for your commencement."

"Nice to meet you. You were looking for me?"

"Yes, I was."

"Wow! That is a surprise!" He hastily added, "A pleasant surprise, of course. My office is right here. Allow me."

He led the way into a room behind the bleachers. Meena looked at the rows of baseball trophies and photographs of teams on the shelves and walls. The coach grinned.

"Yup! A lot of baseball history here."

He removed stuff from a chair.

"Sorry for the mess. Please, take a seat."

He sat on a corner of his desk and waited.

"Coach, I believe you know Professor Madhu Trivedi."

The coach's face visibly tightened.

"Yes, ma'am."

"She was O'Flaherty's teacher."

"Yes."

Meena had to get more than these terse answers. She tried a different tack.

"It must be difficult for your star athletes to keep up in academics."

The frown on the coach's face spoke volumes. He shifted his weight slightly and cleared his throat. Meena knew she had pressed the right button. She leaned back in her chair. Judging from his expression, she'd be here for a while.

"With all due respect to your cousin, ma'am, professors have no inkling what goes on in sports. My boys have to spend each day practicing skills and improving teamwork under my guidance. They train hard and they train relentlessly. Their work hours are often irregular; travel is sometimes extensive. As their coach, I teach them good sportsmanship, a competitive spirit. I am responsible for managing the team during both practice sessions and competitions. Before each competition, I have to evaluate or scout the opposing team to determine game strategies and practice specific plays. My players have very little time for writing assignments — they did enough of those in high school. And every professor thinks his assignment or test or exam or whatever tops everything else. But guess what — collegiate sports drives enrolment. Many of our students come here because of baseball. And of course, increased enrolment makes donors and legislators very happy. Corporations offer money so they can profit from the glory of our college athletes. And our college doesn't seem to have any problem with grabbing all the kudos… And the money! All the profs benefit — they wouldn't see the fantastic pay raises the college gives them without that kind of money."

He stopped abruptly, mopped his face with a small towel, and looked down at her.

"Have to turn down the heat here. Sorry, ma'am, for going on and on about this. It's a sore point with me."

He muttered under his breath, "Eggheads who don't give a damn about sports."

Meena waited for him to calm down.

"You think professors are incapable of imparting real-life education?"

"Yes. No, no, don't misunderstand me, Mrs…. Er… "

"Rao," she prompted.

"Mrs Rao. My apologies. Sure, a college degree is important. But very few students remember the four years' seat time they had to endure once they graduate. They can always get back to book learning later in life if they need to. But now is the time to take advantage of their young bodies. And let us not forget that our athletes bring much greater visibility to the college. All I'm asking for is a little consideration from our educators. A passing grade…"

Meena got up. She forced a smile and allowed him to accompany her back to the Martin Luther King Hall building where she had an appointment with Christopher Reay, Head of the Department of Cultural Studies.

***

Meena perfunctorily thanked Coach Miller and took the elevator up to Christopher Reay's office. As she rounded the corner, she heard footsteps running behind her. She turned around and saw a tall lanky student with a mop of red hair.

"Ms Rao, do you have a moment?"

She waited for him to come up to her.

"My name is Martin McDonald. I am one of Professor Trivedi's students."

"You are the one whose... I mean, who... I am so very sorry for your loss, Martin."

"Thank you, Ms Rao. It hasn't fully sunk in. I wondered... Professor Leela Rao has asked me to meet her tomorrow to discuss... things. But Ignatius' parents have requested me to help them make arrangements for the burial rites — whenever the cops release his body. May I talk to you instead? Of course, if you think that's inappropriate, I could always..."

"No, that would be fine. I can give Leela — Professor Rao — all the details of our conversation. Could you come to Professor Reay's office in half an hour? I have an appointment with him now."

"Of course, Ms Rao. We have a seminar library room around the corner. If that's okay with you, we could talk there."

"Sounds good," Meena assured him and went towards Reay's office.

Christopher Reay glanced at an honour's thesis entitled "Closeted advertising: Homophobia in the Media." An older colleague had given the thesis a C+, and the senior had petitioned the department for a re-evaluation of his work. Reay grunted, read the first paragraph, and decided to pass it on to other younger colleagues. All this homosexuality shit that he kept hearing about — he had no inclination to read about it. Who's advising these kids? They can't think beyond their smartphone asses and so-called social issues — gays, abortion, immigration. One day, someone will yank that safety net from under them — they'll end up flipping burgers in some seedy joint. He thought about his home base: The Department of Chemistry and Biochemistry. When the Department of Cultural Studies had been paralyzed by internal strife and locked in inertia two years ago, President Juarez had placed it in academic receivership and appointed Reay as acting head of the department. Juarez had promised Reay that a formal search for the new head would begin as soon as commencement was over. Reay could hardly wait.

He was about to go out onto the balcony when he heard a knock. Madhu's guest — damn it! I'd forgotten all about her. Well, Chris, put on your worried face. He said: "Come!"

Meena's attire took him by surprise. He had expected something more Eastern exotic than that severe business suit. She reminded him of a distant maiden aunt — the same gauntness, the short grey hair, the string of pearls, even down to the closed-toe pumps.

"Come in, come in, Mrs Rao! Madhu has told me so much about you and your cousin. And of course, we'll soon have the honor of hearing her at our commencement."

"Thank you, Professor Reay."

"Christopher, please!"

"Meena. And thank you for agreeing to see me at such short notice. As you may have heard, Madhu asked us to come up here because of those shocking murders. With your institutional history, you could clarify so much for me."

"Institutional history — I feel so old! Yes, I've been at this college since graduating in 1982. It has been quite a long haul."

Meena smiled.

"Christopher, may I be frank?"

"Yes, please!"

"What is your take on O'Flaherty's murder? Was he involved in anything illegal?"

Where is she going with this? He replied noncommittally: "You know how students are in Ivy League colleges! They're privileged beyond belief. All the luxury cars that you see are theirs. What are you thinking?"

"Well, drugs for one. I hear that's a huge problem… At least that's what my cousin tells me, you know, at her school, the U. of Arizona."

"State universities are much more vulnerable — exposed to drugs and other illegal activities. They don't have the resources we have. I can assure you that we work closely with the Vermont Drug Enforcement Agency. Any student in possession of illegal drugs or their distribution is subject to criminal prosecution. And naturally, it's grounds for dismissal from the college. We have an equally rigorous policy about alcohol consumption."

Meena eyed his red face with quiet amusement. I bet he doesn't mind a daily two pegs of whatever.

"About Ignatius… What was the application process for getting him over to the U.S.?"

"The Biodiversity and Natural Resource Management Center in Harare sends a few students every year to study similar issues here at Anderson. Ignatius was among that select few. I believe three others were also awarded grants, but they were sent to other Little Ivies in the northeast. If you are really interested, our Study Abroad Office would give you more details."

"No, that's not necessary. I was curious. He and Martin were close friends, I believe."

"I just found that out. I had no idea that they had rented an off-campus apartment. Obviously, the Dean of Students would have known about their... friendship."

Meena didn't miss the hesitation, nor did she miss the look of distaste on his face. *Can't hide your homophobia very well, can you, my friend!*

"Martin must be devastated. How is he taking it?"

"There are confidentiality issues involved, as you can understand, Meena."

You don't know. And you don't care.

"Of course! I'm sorry I brought it up. Well, I've taken up enough of your time."

They shook hands and Meena thought she heard a soft sigh of relief as she left the room. What was it with these men? They all seemed to be hiding something. She couldn't wait to talk all this over with Leela. She turned a corner and entered the seminar library room.

"Mrs Rao! Here!"

Martin came out from behind one of the stacks.

"Thank you for meeting me. Not many students use this library, which is why I like to come here."

"Martin, you have something significant to tell us. Let's not waste any time."

"Yes. Right. This was something that happened about a week or so ago. Ignatius, another friend Sheila, and I were going to the movies."

"Yes?"

Leela had already told her about Sheila and the man who had accosted Ignatius. But she thought it was important that she hear Martin's version.

"And suddenly this stranger ran up to Ignatius. There seemed to be a heated exchange. Then Ignatius asked Sheila and me to carry on, that he would catch up with us. The strange thing is, he never did come. When we came out of the theater, there he was waiting for us. He looked scared to death. I quizzed him later, tried to find out what had happened. He just said it was an acquaintance. He invented a headache to explain away his tension."

"He said the stranger was an acquaintance from Harare?"

"Yes."

"Can you describe him in greater detail?"

"No. I really couldn't make out anything. This is winter in Vermont, Ms Rao. He was tall, but the coat, earmuffs, hat, and scarf covered every part of his body. Also, I'm assuming it was a man because of the height."

"Well, too bad. Anything else?"

Martin shook his head as he sadly stroked a pendant that hung from a silver chain around his neck. Meena looked at it and fleetingly thought: That is an interesting design! Where have I seen it before?

March 23: A hoodie is sent home

Dr Michael Borden looked at the list of belongings taken from the corpse:

1. Pair of shabby jeans
2. Soiled white shirt
3. Black woollen hoodie
4. Rolex

Dr Borden paused. A Rolex? On a homeless guy? Must have stolen it. Didn't have time to hock it. He read on:

5. Loose change
6. One ten-dollar bill
7. Bracelet and matching earrings

A bracelet and matching earrings… What? Could be part of a jewellery heist. He opened the cardboard box containing all the items and lifted out the bracelet. It looked very expensive — to his untutored eye, it seemed like solid silver. There was something engraved on the clasp. A design of some kind. He'd have to use his magnifying glass. But first, he'd have the Rolex and bracelet traced, and ask the local police to look into recent robberies.

March 23: Sarducci's again

Madhu had thought long and hard before saying 'yes' to a second dinner invitation. She was undeniably attracted to Charles. He had been knowledgeable about a wide range of topics without the accompanying arrogance that most of the men she had dated displayed. When he had called the following morning to ask her out again, she had insisted that she be the one to pick up the check. He had promptly agreed, which had been yet another point in his favor. She had also told him that she would pick him up in her modest Mini Cooper Coupe. She had detected a smile in his voice when he had responded with "Of course, Madhu."

Charles had chosen European clothing. The modest lines of the suit pleased her. *But I'm sure he didn't buy it at Burlington Coat Factory! Must be something from London — one of those haute couture joints on Savile Row.* She wore a lightweight Kashmiri silk sari that her father had chosen for her first sari-wearing 'ceremony'. She remembered the day so clearly, it brought tears to her eyes. Father had insisted on coming along when her mother took her to a fashionable clothing store. After what seemed like hundreds of saris later, she had wanted to leave. But her father had unerringly pointed to a sari that still lay folded on a shelf. She had immediately fallen in love with it; the colours had taken her breath away, from the Persian green of the border to the contrasting teal of the body.

The maître d' remembered them, led them to the same table as before and placed the wine list in front of Charles.

"This is too corny!" she smiled. "And now he'll play 'our song', I suppose."

Charles grinned mischievously.

"My, my! Aren't we a wee bit touchy!"

She grinned in return.

"Forget it! I will not allow even the slightest sign of sexism to spoil this evening."

An hour later, the waiter brought around two steaming cups of cappuccino. Madhu sat back and sighed.

"You sound less stressed out," Charles said, leaning across the table.

"I do? That's good."

"Those murders still bothering you?"

"Yes and no. I wish I could wipe out that look of hopelessness on Martin's face. You know, my student whose Zimbabwean partner was murdered."

"Ignatius, right?"

"Yes."

"What about the athlete? The baseball player?"

"The police have been keeping a tight lid on everything."

"What do they say?"

"Well, they don't know yet," Madhu replied morosely. "Beheading is very likely to be Al-Qaeda's calling card, the MO of Islamist terrorists. Remember Daniel Pearl's beheading by Khalid Sheikh Mohammed in Pakistan."

Madhu groaned.

"Oh! Yes, I see what you mean! I don't know. I can't think straight any more."

Charles called the waiter.

"Two Rémy Martin, please!"

Madhu sat up straight.

"Are you trying to get me tipsy, Mr Charles Nandoro? Then let me assure you that you are succeeding marvellously!"

March 23: The cousins confer with the chief

In pure gold inlay on the sword-guards
there were rune-markings correctly
incised. (Beowulf, lines 1694-1695)
Beowulf took a firm hold of the hilt
and swung the blade in an arc, a resolute
blow that bit deep into her neck-bone
and severed it entirely, toppling the
doomed house of her flesh; she fell
to the floor. The sword dripped blood,
the swordsman was elated.

(Beowulf, lines 1564–1569)[10]

Chief Inspector Bonnie Martel looked at the two seventy-six-year-old women with wonder in her eyes and a pleased smile.

---

[10] Beowulf: An Old English epic poem consisting of 3,182 alliterative long lines, set in Scandinavia, the oldest surviving epic poem of Old English and thus commonly cited as one of the most important works of Anglo-Saxon literature, and also arguably the earliest vernacular English literature. (http://en.wikipedia.org/wiki/Beowulf)

"Let me guess — you are really undercover FBI agents, aren't you, just pretending to be sweet old ladies?"

The cousins smiled complacently.

"Well," Martel went on, "all the info you've brought me is extremely useful. I'll have to go over everything carefully with my assistants. But I have something too for you, ladies," she added triumphantly. "I just received this from the Chittenden County Regional Forensic Crime Lab."

She opened a cardboard box and took out a solid silver bracelet.

"A young man was found executed Chicago-style in Cabot, Vermont, in a cheese cave of all places! His fingerprints were fortunately available on AFIS — Automated Fingerprint Identification System. The man had a juvenile record and several priors. They identified him as one Mohammed Iqbal of Benson, Rutland County, twenty-eight years old. Jailed half a dozen times for petty larceny. Parents are immigrants, came to the U.S. in the '80s from Saudi Arabia. Mohammed Iqbal was born in Benson. Quite harmless really, so why would anybody want to execute him? He might have bitten off more than he could chew this time. The ME also found drugs in his body and several needle marks on his arms Anyway, what I wanted to show you was this symbol. What does it remind you of?"

Leela and Meena took the bracelet and peered at it.

Meena exclaimed, "This is… I saw this design recently. Now, where…?"

Leela fingered the bracelet.

"It is heavy. Must have cost the earth!"

"Yes. I'm sure he took it off one of the bodies to give it possibly to a fence!" Martel commented. She looked at Meena who had sat down and was lost in thought.

"She gets like that — quite often," Leela explained. "Let's give her a couple of minutes."

A minute later, Meena looked up, saw the two faces staring expectantly at her, and smiled.

"I've got it. I mean, I know where I saw that design — on a pendant. Martin McDonald wears a silver chain, and the pendant has the exact same design. I wish I had my book on religious symbols, the one you insist on using as a weight to flatten things out! But perhaps we can find something online. Chief Martel, may I…?"

She took the chief's laptop and rapidly typed in: *Hall & Puleston, Illustrated Dictionary of Symbols in Eastern and Western Art*. She clicked on the 'Look inside' caption and scrolled through the images.

"Here it is! Look!"

She pointed to a symbol under the chapter on Buddhist symbols.

"It's the chakra showing the noble eightfold paths. Arabic calligraphy, Buddhist chakras... This is becoming a multicultural nightmare!"

Leela piped up, "But what I can't figure out is how a petty larcenist would resort to such violence! It's out of character. I mean, bludgeoning the victim to death, then decapitating him? Why behead him?"

Meena explained, "Death by the blade is about shame, suffering in an animal slaughterhouse. Muslims and Christians alike have shared this belief. Germanic customs bear witness to such practices. And the practice was continued when the guillotine began chopping heads more efficiently..."

She looked up.

"Or perhaps the real killer used Mohammed Iqbal because of the latter's presumed ability to write Arabic? Chief Inspector, didn't you mention that the murder weapon was the same in both cases?"

Bonnie Martel responded cautiously, "Well, that's what both autopsies revealed. But in her examination of the severed head and torso in order to determine what kind of knife had been used, the ME saw something weird. When she examined the wound, she discovered a gold tip. Who would forge a blade out of gold? She also performed a forensic reconstruction with the lab's three-dimensional graphics and computer simulation system, gauging the length, weight, and curvature of the weapon from the cut itself. The image she created from the simulation system is interesting. Here, look at it."

Martel handed the cousins a couple of photographs of the image the ME had made. Leela looked at her cousin.

"Meena, what do you think?"

"This looks very much like a Shamshir, a type of curved sabre. I'll have to investigate it some more. But I doubt that Shamshirs have been used in recent times."

"Recent times... Hmmm! What exactly does that mean, Ms Rao?"

Meena looked at her cousin.

"Remember, Leela, the reading we did before going to Istanbul?"

"Well, you did the reading, as I recollect!"

"Okay. But I do remember reading about the collection of weaponry in the Topkapı Palace. And we saw some beautiful exemplars of Shamshirs in the museum there. What puzzles me is the gold tip! Normally, only the handles would have been forged out of gold, and the actual sword would be made of carbon steel."

Martel said, "You're implying that someone attached a gold tip to the original sword. Of course, that doesn't surprise me. My father is a collector of firearms from the American frontier; he has a pretty eclectic collection of European-made arms — Webley, Adams, Enfield. The pride of his collection is a gold-plated Browning Hi-Power 9mm handgun that once belonged to Muammar Gaddafi. Apparently, Gaddafi couldn't forget his Bedouin roots and embellished the tribal weapons with gold! Our killer might have taken similar liberties with his collection."

She got up.

"Oh! I forgot to mention. The ME's detailed analysis of the gold tip turned up something very interesting. It was made of twenty-two karat gold. My own research shows that many countries in the Middle East are less rigid about indicating gold purity with a stamp. This gold tip should have displayed the stamp '916' or '917' to signify twenty-two karats, which it didn't. Our initial assumption about the killer having connections to the Middle East is now further strengthened."

"In India, people usually insist on twenty-two karat, too," Leela observed. She noticed that Meena sat silently, running her fingers through her short hair. Chief Martel looked enquiringly at Leela.

"She is doing it again, Chief, sorting things out in her mind! She'll tell us soon enough."

Meena began, "The Arabic calligraphy, the beheading, and now the gold tip — all pointing away from the U.S. — it seems staged, ritualistically staged to blame radicalism. This is all too deliberate, too facile. Misdirection. I... I don't like it one bit. The two murders are connected, I'm positive, but not in this way. There is something else, and someone is doing his or her best to distract us from it."

March 24: Madhu confides in the cousins

"He's gallant and intelligent, and beautiful, and..."

"Okay! Say no more! Well, you have the... What do you youngsters say? ...The 'hots' for him."

The cousins chuckled as Leela polished off the last Gulab-jamun[11] that Madhu had bought that morning.

"Tell us all, child!"

"Well, nothing to tell... Yet!" Her eyes twinkled. "You old rogues! You're matchmaking! I have no intention to... That is, I like him a lot of course. He's very interested in the murders. It helps me talk about them with him. Hey! There you go again making me talk about him! Back to you — what have you found out?"

"Your Meena aunty thinks all the leads we have so far are bogus. Everything is misdirection. Madhu, we have to continue talking to the people here on and off campus. Your students are our best bet. You and I could talk some more with them."

Meena said, "I'll dig more thoroughly into the backgrounds of your Dean of Students and Coach

---

[11] A milk-solids based dessert, similar to a dumpling.

Miller. They are hiding something. By the way, I don't know how you can tolerate your head of department. Christopher Reay is a sexist and a homophobe."

Madhu laughed.

"That's putting it mildly! He's a pain, but we're getting a new head soon. The reason Reay became head is because this department was a mess two years ago, just before I came on board. Our president euphemistically termed it 'internal strife.' But it was in fact a violent confrontation between the previous head and a prof who has since retired."

"What was the fight about?"

"A study abroad program in Africa — Zimbabwe! Zimbabwe! Why is it cropping up everywhere? Well, this older professor had started the program, initiated contacts with Zimbabwe Open University, Women's University in Africa, and the Midlands State University. Anderson College was supposed to send six sophomores that first year, two to each school. But then the head had his own list of candidates, the kids of rich business buddies of his. Merit went out of the window. The prof discovered email correspondence between the head and the parents of these kids, negotiating substantial amounts of money as bribes. He lost no time exposing the head; the department practically shut down, and President Carlos Juarez fired him, took the department under receivership, and brought Reay in."

Leela said, "That reminds me — we have to request Chief Martel to check the financials of the 'terrible trio' — Dean, Head, and Coach."

March 24: A deal goes sour

Coach Jeb Miller looked at his list of names. He hadn't been able to meet the quota for this month. The payoff would be painfully small. He had to find some more volunteers. Hopefully, April would be better. A fresh batch was expected in a couple of weeks. He backed out of the garage and drove to the *McMoran Advisors International* head office in Montpelier. The conference hall was full as he entered. He took his usual seat closest to the door and anxiously looked around for his contact from the cartel. He took out the small black bag from his duffel bag and looked inside. He hadn't been able to get rid of the whole consignment. His contact wouldn't be too happy. He rubbed his eyes. It had been a long, exhausting night with his wife screaming at him, "I'll kill her; I'll kill that whore! I've had enough. You get rid of her, or else…"

He'd have to do something. The new volunteers might turn the tide. He'd have to pressure some of the small-time brokers in his pay to increase distribution. The contact sat down quietly next to him. Miller felt a prick in his side. No one noticed two men leaving the hall, one of them leaning heavily on the other.

March 24: Edifying conversations

Charles Swinburne breathed rapidly. He had shot up a couple of hours ago. What was it that the dealer had called it? Afro-something. That was funny! His mouth felt dry. But he couldn't get up. He needed some more of the stuff. Where was his cell? Had to make a call — quickly. Someone was knocking. Who the hell…? The door opened, and that geek from his math class stuck his head in.

"Hey, dude! You have a VI-SI-TORR!"

Swinburne dragged himself to the restroom, splashed water on his face, and made his way to the visitors' lounge. It was that woman again, that old prof from Arizona.

"At ease, Swinburne," Leela said, noting the twitch that he was trying to hide. He looked worn out, more so than last time.

"Swinburne, you don't look well."

"No, Prof… Professor, I'm fine. I'm fine. No problem. Ask away."

He went up to the water cooler and rapidly drained a couple of glasses.

"You told me last time that Sean O'Flaherty was dealing in drugs."

Swinburne nodded his head.

"Was that common knowledge?"

Swinburne took a deep breath. He had to get rid of the woman quickly. *To hell with Sean!*

"I… You know how it is. Everybody does it… That is, everybody is in on it. You know how it is. I… I don't think I should… Don't think I can say more."

He got up. *Face is flushed, breathing rapid.*

"All right, Swinburne. Make sure you call me if you think of anything you want to tell me. Here is my cell number."

She had hardly stepped outside the room when Swinburne punched in a number on his cell. Leela listened intently outside the room. 2… 2… 3… 2… 2… 4… 3… Gotcha! Cousin Meena had an angelic voice, but Leela's ears had perfect pitch too. She took out her own cell and entered the number under 'contacts.' She would go back to Madhu's home and place the call.

***

Sheila Gilmore entered the visitors' lounge of her dorm.

"Professor Rao, what a surprise! I'm, like, so glad you came back. You have more, like, questions for me, right?"

"That's right, Sheila. We are urgently looking for more leads. Who knows when that killer might strike again?"

"Yes, yes. You know, it's, like, strange that you should say that. Iggy, Ignatius... He said the same thing. It was, like, the day before he was..."

"What did he say, Sheila? Try to remember his exact words, if you can."

Vertical lines of concentration appeared on the student's brow.

"He said, 'We must... We must stop it.' Yes! That's what he said! I know coz I said, like, 'Stop what, Iggy?'"

"Anything else you can remember?"

Sheila shook her head despondently.

"Thank you, Sheila. This has been more helpful than you can imagine. Don't give up! We'll track that monster down."

***

Martin looked at his lover's books and clothes one last time. Shona rituals dictated that they be buried with Iggy. He replayed the discussion he had just had with Iggy's father. Mr Munyaradzi had proceeded to describe the last rites. Customarily, when a person came to die at home, Shona elders who were in the company of the deceased during his/her last hours saw to it that a ritual called Kupeta (folding) was performed.

"But in our son's case, it is different. In the last letter that he wrote to us," Mr Munyaradzi confessed with tears in his eyes, "Ignatius told us that this apartment that he shares with you was his home. Chief Inspector Martel has assured me that the ME will respect our son — your partner — in every way. The eyes will be closed, hands and legs straightened, and placed in the right posture for burial. You and I, we will then ritually wash and anoint him, after which he will be ceremoniously wrapped in a new cloth of blanket and then laid on a reed sleeping mat in a coffin."

He placed a gentle hand on Martin's shoulder.

"It will bring you peace, my son. Our elders have not prescribed all these rituals for nothing. There is comfort in them; there is harmony in them. There is a Shona saying:

> *An ancestral spirit is like a bird; it abandons the*
> *one who abuses it.*
> *A united family eats from the same plate*
> *Hold a true friend with both hands*
> *Where there is love there is no darkness."*

He stopped and looked at Martin's desolate face. "There is also a Buddhist saying…"

"Buddhist?" Martin asked, "You knew, sir?"

"Yes, son, I knew. Ignatius was different in so many ways. Some of them we just couldn't comprehend. But he was a good…"

He wiped tears from his eyes.

"He was a good son and a good human being. Even before he came to the U.S., I knew of his longing for alternate spiritual paths. He had already turned to Buddhist philosophy."

He looked attentively at Martin.

"Sit down, my son. Let me give you some background on your partner, my son. You know a little about Zimbabwe, but let me provide you with some more insights into why Ignatius came to the U.S."

He sat down, rubbed his eyes once again, and continued.

"Some years ago, about a decade after Robert Mugabe was elected prime minister, some of us intellectuals formed an oppositional group to fight what was increasingly becoming an authoritarian government. Mugabe and his North Korean goons, the so-called Fifth Brigade began terrorizing the whole country. He called us dissidents 'born again colonialists'! His reign of terror now extends beyond our own borders to those Zimbabweans living in the diaspora, especially those in the US. Your President's economic sanctions a couple of years ago have led to the disappearance of dozens of Zimbabweans — probably kidnapped and murdered by members of the Fifth Brigade. When Ignatius was growing up, everyone worshipped Mugabe as a hero — and rightly so. After all, Mugabe had fought a seven-year guerrilla war against Rhodesia's white-led government. But then his increasing despotic behaviour affected everyone."

He paused and took a sip of water.

"Martin, my son, we both know that Ignatius was an extraordinary boy. He discovered his homosexuality very early — he told me later that he must have been about twelve or thirteen. And boys in his school began to harass him, call him names. He must have felt so alone, so much an outsider of society. When he graduated from high school, he suddenly began discussing religion with me. I saw him one day reading a book about Buddhism. I had heard of the Buddha of course, but in Zimbabwe, our syncretism extends only to Shona and Christianity. His newfound interest coincided with your visit to our country."

"Yes, sir. I had already begun a shift to Buddhism. I believe that all religious beliefs have their roots in compassion. But I felt that Christianity had lost this quality. Of course, its condemnatory attitude towards gays made it imperative that I turn to other possibilities. Ignatius was experiencing a similar crisis in identity and faith. I don't think it had to do with the Shona belief system, but rather with the Mugabe government's blatant homophobia."

Mr Munyaradzi smiled sadly.

"The Buddha's words, ones that Ignatius recited so often, speak to the concerns and search for spiritual paths that both of you shared:

"In the end
these things matter most:
How well did you love?

How fully did you live?
How deeply did you let go?

After the rituals here, we hope — Ignatius' mother and I — that you will come back to Harare with us for a family gathering to mourn Ignatius' passing on the soil of his birth."

"About the ritual, sir…"

"Please! I am your father — by law, but nevertheless your father."

"Father, about the ritual — you know that Buddhists cremate their dead."

Mr Munyaradzi clasped Martin's hand.

"After we have completed our Shona rituals, my son — your partner — will be cremated."

March 24: More bodies surface

Coach Jeb Miller's wife was not worried about his absence. The fool must have gone to that tart's place. She poured herself a glass of bourbon, rolled a joint, and made herself comfortable on the couch before switching the TV on. "The Real Housewives of Orange County" was on.

She had fallen out of love early in their marriage and would have left Jeb but for the drug money that provided many a luxury, including the expensive Bourbon she was now consuming. What a schmuck! She was biding her time. Once the well was dry, she would move on. But first, she would take him and that floozy of his to the cleaners. She took a deep drag from the joint, drank a third of the Bourbon, and snuggled more deeply into the plush cushions. She heard a thud. He must be back. Well, he'd follow his usual pattern — swear drunkenly at her, and collapse in the guestroom that had become his bedroom for years now.

They had begun this relationship of ignoring each other years ago once the doctor had diagnosed Jeb with low sperm count. The doctor had called it 'oligospermia.' She burst into raucous laughter. A fancy name didn't make him more of a man! A total lack of common interests compounded by a childless marriage had led even more quickly to estrangement. She took another massive gulp of Bourbon. *One more joint won't hurt.* She had just finished rolling it when a loud crash made her jump. What the hell was that? Must be drunk, the jerk. Slipped in his puke. Not my problem. She returned to the couch. She removed the sweater that she had put on earlier. She was sweating! Was it those damn hot flushes again? The room felt much warmer. She began coughing. She saw dense smoke seeping into the room from under the door leading to the basement. It rapidly filled the room. She ran to the door, lunged forward as it collapsed, and fell down the stairs into a roaring wall of fire.

***

Montpelier, VT — March 25, 2006

The home of Coach Jeb Miller was burnt down around midnight last night. Police suspect arson. Two bodies charred beyond recognition were found in the basement. The fire had been raging for a while before neighbours called 911. Anderson College has been having more than its share of tragedies this semester: the brutal killing of star quarterback Sean O'Flaherty, followed by the murder of an exchange student from Zimbabwe.

Police have not confirmed reports that the bodies are those of Coach Miller and his wife Agnes. The extent of damage to the house is not known yet, but reliable sources told this reporter that nothing could be salvaged.

March 25: "Parting is such sweet sorrow"

"How long will you be gone?"

"I can't say. It might be a week or so. It's business, McMoran business. I'm lucky to have had a couple of weeks free of travel!"

Madhu didn't respond.

"Madhu? Madhu, are you there?"

"Yes, Charles. I'm here. Where are you off to?"

"Tomorrow morning, I fly to Cape Town. After that, it's anybody's guess. I have to check with my… Secretary — it depends on the availability of some of the businessmen there."

He laughed.

"African business negotiations run on a different concept of time. It is considered impolite to dive straight into business discussions. One has to enquire about family and so forth."

"Oh!" Madhu had to laugh. "Just like in India. When I worked at the Marriott in Minnesota, they were in the middle of negotiations with Indian hoteliers about opening a branch of Marriott in Mumbai. And they complained endlessly to me about the Indians' 'unwillingness to come to the point,' as they put it."

"Well, yes. It is very much the same in most African countries."

Madhu heard whispering over the phone. Charles said rather abruptly, "Have to go, Madhu. I'll call you when I get back."

She slipped the cell into her coat pocket and sat back. The whispering — what was that all about? She got up with a groan — her overactive imagination always got her into trouble! She picked up her briefcase and left the office. It was Saturday. She entered a near-empty parking lot. The only other car in the lot was one of those flashy sports models. She could make out the colour — too loud for a car! *Aunties will be waiting. Got to get home.* She threw her briefcase onto the rear seat of her car and drove away.

She breathed in the wonderful aroma of freshly brewed coffee as she entered her apartment.

"You are real pets!" she said, setting down her briefcase and hugging first one, then the other cousin. "And samosas,[12] too! You remembered! When Murali broke the news about Mom to me, he reminded me how all of us — Rahul, Raman, Sarada, Parvathi, Surya — would race to my house from school just for Mom's scrumptious samosas. And I would beat them all ... and always get that extra samosa, although mom scolded me for being so greedy!"

---

[12] Fried or baked pastry with a savory filling, such as spiced potatoes, onions, peas, cheese, beef and other meats, or lentils.

Meena Rao smiled. Her twin boys, Rahul and Raman, weren't the athletic types. Her daughter, Sarada, was older than the rest and had considered herself above such childishness, although that hadn't stopped her from grabbing her share of samosas. Leela's daughter Parvathi and son Surya had both inherited their mother's sweet tooth. Madhu's mother, Komal, had never hesitated to pander to it. The kids had grown up, almost overnight it seemed to her now, and vanished to various parts of the globe. Only Murali and Meghna had remained in Tucson.

Coffee and several samosas later, the three looked at each other.

"Now what?" Meena said, echoing the thoughts of the others.

"We have nothing! Our prime suspect has been executed, a — what would the police call him? — a 'person of interest' has been burnt to death, and we have nothing but speculation. Is it a terrorist agenda, are drugs involved, are the two murders related, and if so, what is the connection? And if the young man found in that cheese cave was a hired assassin, who hired him? And what about Coach Miller's death? What about a motive for the arson? From your accounts of the coach, Madhu, and Meena, he was a very unpleasant character. But unpleasantness doesn't necessarily end in murder."

Leela's quick summary reminded them of all the questions that remained unanswered.

"What about the African Studies Department? Won't it be helpful to talk to some of the members there? Or to the professor who was Ignatius' advisor?"

Madhu jumped up.

"It's Saturday! Of course. Come on! I'll take you there. Every Saturday, students and faculty get together in the departmental residential hall. It's very informal and a lot of fun. Everyone will be relaxed. Perfect for you old snoops!"

Loud music and laughter greeted them as they neared the residential hall. Madhu led the cousins straight to Anthony Chikwava, head of the Department of African Studies.

"Anthony, hi! I'd like you to meet two ladies who have been my role models ever since I grew out of diapers!"

A stout man in his late sixties got up with a broad smile. He brushed pastry crumbs from his short-sleeved guayabera shirt[13] and extended a hand covered with diamond rings to the women.

"Word gets around, word gets around! Professor Rao, we knew about your extraordinary scholarly achievements, extraordinary scholarly achievements when we invited you to be our commencement speaker. A real pleasure to finally meet you! A real pleasure! And Mrs Rao, welcome as well. You two have revealed

---

[13] Safari shirt or shirt-jac.

talents most unusual, most unusual! Detecting — I would never have guessed, never have guessed."

"Such charming flattery will get you everywhere, Professor Chikwava!" Leela chuckled delightedly. "About Ignatius — we will get the monster who did it sooner or later. He or she is bound to slip up. Meena and I have seen it happen again and again. Even the most brilliant criminal minds make mistakes."

"Well, all I can say is that I fervently hope, fervently hope you catch those killers, dear ladies. Ignatius was a treasure, a treasure. He is sorely missed."

Meena nodded.

"I can imagine. Professor Chikwava…"

"Please call me Anthony!"

"Anthony, what can you tell us about Ignatius?" Chikwava offered his guests a plate of African pastries while he gathered his thoughts.

"I would recommend the Brik," he said, pointing to stuffed pastry from Algeria. "And the Briouat — Moroccan — is also most delicious, most delicious. One of our students just brought it back from Fez. Well, about Ignatius — where should I begin, where should I begin? He came to us through the good offices of our president Carlos Juarez. Carlos is an Africanist himself. I should say 'was'."

He smiled ironically.

"The high offices of the presidency don't leave much time, much time for more scholarly endeavours. To come back to Ignatius. He was quite fluent, quite fluent in Shona, and taught the rudiments of the language to a number of our students. I found out that he was remarkably well-informed, remarkably well-informed about Shona spiritual beliefs. Ignatius became an informal mentor, an informal mentor to one of our undergraduates who wanted to write a thesis on African religious practices, African religious practices."

Leela and Meena looked at each other, confounded by Anthony's weirdly echoing speech pattern. He took a sip of wine and continued.

"I myself had several discussions, several discussions with him about religions, especially Buddhism. Interestingly, he told me that he had seriously considered, seriously considered becoming a Bhikkhu,[14] that is, before he met Martin McDonald."

He added with a grin, "I think his plans to lead a life of celibacy… Ha-ha! A life of celibacy vanished right about then."

"Did his sexual orientation make him enemies?"

"Not to my knowledge, not to my knowledge. The students at Anderson are pretty open-minded, pretty open-minded. But one never knows. Ah yes! There was this one incident of hate mail, posted on his locker, a typewritten note saying: 'Gays are worse than dogs and pigs.' That was a quote, a quote from the man who calls himself the president, the president of Zimbabwe —

---

[14] An ordained male Buddhist monk.

Robert Mugabe. We had another incident of hate mail, our student from Egypt… Excuse me, ladies!"

He turned to greet a couple of students who had come up to him. The cousins walked away to mingle. An hour later, they met up near the bar with Madhu.

Leela ordered a tall Shirley Temple and took a huge gulp of what Meena condemned as 'that saccharine, sweet, icky drink'. She gave a huge sigh of satisfaction and said, "Everybody loved him! Has excessive love ever killed? No, don't answer that!"

She gulped down some more of the sweet beverage.

"I spoke to Ignatius' mentor, Professor Lahra Mendenhall. She is an Associate Professor, a cultural anthropologist; she told me she 'works' on the Ndebele people in Zimbabwe! For her, Ignatius was every anthropologist's dream — a native informant, ready to present 'untainted' information about his culture. Well, we have had our share of 'brown sahibs' in post-colonial India who have no other agenda than to self-promote in the Western world."

Madhu helped herself to a glass of Merlot and took a wary sip.

"Yuck! When will I ever learn not to drink wine served at college functions?"

She wiped her mouth and returned the glass to the counter.

"That's a pretty accurate portrayal. You amaze me, Leela aunty. Lahra Mendenhall is one of those anthropologists who see 'subjects' from the 'third' world as fair game. They set out to destroy the vocal cords of the 'represented' people! I didn't have much success either. Everyone is wary of saying anything to me."

A silent Meena sat on one of the bar stools sipping a pink lemonade. Leela jabbed a plump finger into her cousin's side.

"Hey! Cousin! Come back, come back from wherever you are!"

"Ouch!" came the response. "Do you have to…"

She looked at the two women.

"I think I might have discovered something. Madhu, do you know a student by the name of Mariah Wilson?"

Madhu shook her head.

"What about her?"

"She is a Buddhist, like Martin. In fact, she knows… knew Ignatius very well — they attended meditation sessions together. She wore a necklace with the same Buddhist chakra pendant. There was something she had been meaning to tell Martin but wasn't sure how he'd take it."

They waited while she took a sip of water.

"They — she was with Martin and Ignatius — had just attended a session on Vajrayana Buddhism, and were walking back to the department when Ignatius took a call on his cell. She remembers his voice, how frightened it sounded. He wouldn't tell them, not even Martin, what it was about. Before they walked into their next class, Ignatius excused himself and said he had to go to the men's room. Apparently, he didn't come back till much later."

"Did she find out what the call was about?"

"No. It seems that Ignatius told Martin it was a Shona matter. Mariah said that Martin could never bring himself to probe when Ignatius brought out the family card. But Martin was really worried. When Ignatius was murdered, Martin took his phone."

"Ah!" Leela exclaimed. "That explains why the cops didn't find it on him."

"He scrolled through numbers rather absentmindedly and noticed that there were several calls from one particular number. When he called that number on an impulse, it went to voicemail — a professional voicemail greeting. Mariah says she was there with him when he called the number. The number looked familiar, so she made a mental note of it. She wrote this down from memory."

Meena showed them a slip of paper. Madhu said, "It's a college number. Most of our office numbers begin with 828. I can easily check to whom this belongs."

She called the college operator.

"It belongs to the office of the Department Head of African Studies, Professor Anthony Chikwava," she was told. "His administrative assistant and he share the number."

137

March 26: Inhumane business

He pushed the luggage cart to the waiting stretch limousine. The liveried chauffeur jumped out, tipped his hat, took the cart from him, and opened the door.

"The usual, sir?" the chauffeur enquired.

"Yes."

He opened the minibar and poured himself a shot of single malt whisky. Opening his laptop, he rapidly scrolled through rows of numbers. The limo slowed down and stopped in front of a rundown hotel. Children playing hopscotch on the street stopped in their tracks at the sight of such opulence. A figure emerged from the hotel, quickly opened the door, and handed him a briefcase.

"They're getting too close. Montpelier is nervous. We have to move quickly."

"I'll take care of it," he said. "Tell the others to keep to their schedules."

The chauffeur waited for the figure to get away from the limo before speeding away. The man at the back could see the lights of the stadium in the distance. The game would begin in half an hour. He had been cleared to meet the players beforehand. The chauffeur drove the vehicle to the rear of the stadium.

"You will wait here. Use this on anybody who comes too close."

He handed the chauffeur a gun with a silencer.

"Understood, sir!"

A half-hour later, the man was back in the limo. They drove to the airport. A private jet waited on the tarmac. His cell buzzed.

"Yes, I'm on my way back. Begin shredding. …Don't be idiotic! They have no evidence. Just keep your head! Meet me at the usual place."

He thoughtfully slipped the phone into the inside pocket of his Gieves & Hawkes Bespoke quilted parka.

***

Chief Inspector Bonnie Martel looked at the files for the umpteenth time. What was she missing? There was something in the file, in the photos the CSI had taken. The trace evidence at both scenes was consistent with the deaths having occurred at these locations where they were found. Was there anything unusual about the evidence? She shook her head. The autopsy report on Sean O'Flaherty showed no signs of drug abuse, only clear signs of alcoholism. She glanced at the text when suddenly a phrase caught her eye: 'traces of anal fissure'.

Fissure… A crack? Perhaps the result of constipation? She imagined that the high-protein diet that most athletes followed would lead to constipation.

She looked at the autopsy report on Ignatius Munyaradzi. Interesting! The words 'traces of anal fissure' occurred here as well. Best to ask the ME what 'fissure' meant. She took out her cell.

"Hi, Dr Burton, this is Bonnie Martel. Yes, thank you. In fact, I have the reports in front of me. A quick question: what is the 'anal fissure' you noticed during your autopsy of Sean O'Flaherty and Ignatius Munyaradzi? I see… Trauma. Oh! It could also have been caused by the insertion of a foreign object… Like a rectal thermometer? Thanks a lot."

She sat back chewing the end of a ballpoint. Her cell buzzed.

"Chief Martel, there's something we need to discuss. Can we come over now?"

Ten minutes later, the cousins and Madhu sat in Martel's office. Martel listened intently as they told her about Mariah Wilson and the telephone number.

"The head of the Department of African Studies? Hard to believe! I'll have him brought in for questioning."

Leela Rao cautioned, "He's from Zimbabwe, says he doesn't favour the regime there. But that might be just a ruse."

Meena Rao cleared her throat.

"There are some others we haven't yet questioned — Ignatius' parents."

Chief Martel looked curiously at Meena.

"They are, of course, anxiously waiting for the ME to release their son's body."

"I understand, Chief Inspector. But I would very much like to talk to them if you don't mind."

"Be my guest, Mrs Rao!"

***

Meena spotted Mr and Mrs Munyaradzi in the lobby of their hotel sipping hot tea. Munyaradzi stood up when he noticed Meena approaching them.

"Mrs Rao, please join us. A cup of tea?"

Meena nodded and sat down at the table.

"Thank you for agreeing to meet me. Please accept my apologies for intruding at such a time. I cannot begin to imagine what you are going through."

Mrs Munyaradzi placed a hand on Meena's.

"We know that you and your cousin, Professor Rao, are helping the police find our son's killer. If there is anything we can do to help... Sitting around like this is... I don't think I can bear it much longer."

Meena choked for a moment. Losing a child to such violence was inconceivable. What could she possibly do to lessen their grief?

"You can help, Mr and Mrs Munyaradzi. We are trying to find a motive. If there is anything, anything at all that would help us figure out why this happened... "

The couple looked at each other. Mr Munyaradzi took a deep breath and began.

"There is something we have been too ashamed to share with anyone here, Mrs Rao. May God forgive us! We just wanted our child to get away from Zimbabwe before they got to him."

"Who?"

"The North Korean goons, the so-called Fifth Brigade, hired by Mugabe…"

"President Mugabe?"

"Forgive me, Mrs Rao, but we consider it offensive to use that title. Mugabe's anti-gay crusade would have ultimately targeted our son. But we didn't have the resources to send Ignatius out of the country. There was only one way…"

He crossed himself.

"A way that was abhorrent to us but would at least take him out of the reach of the killers in our country."

"Illegal?" Meena asked.

"Criminal. Acquaintances told us about a drug ring operating out of Harare. They recruited young men and women as drug mules."

"Drug mules? I have heard of them. But what exactly do they do?"

"They carry drugs inserted into their bodies that they later eject through a bowel movement. Drug packets — usually cocaine, heroin, or methamphetamine — are compressed to be as dense as possible, and placed into some kind of latex. The packet might also include aluminium foil or something similar to avoid detection by a machine."

Meena grew pale.

"Your son?"

"Yes. He insisted. The contact promised to pay the full fare and all expenses for expediting the application process for a passport and visa. In return, Ignatius would carry drugs to a prestigious college on the east coast of the U.S. He was chosen for Anderson College."

"Drug dealers in Harare have been infiltrating rich colleges in the U.S.," Mrs Munyaradzi added. "We were assured that this was a one-time deal, that Ignatius would be released from any further obligations once he passed the drugs on to a contact in Montpelier."

"But it didn't stop there, did it?"

"No, it didn't! We were blinded by our concern for our son. Drug dealers are ruthless. We should have realized that. We didn't know that they continued to abuse our son in the U.S. Ignatius didn't tell us about it until recently."

"Why did he wait so long?"

"He wanted to stop. But they told him they would kill us if he didn't 'cooperate'. As long as we were in Zimbabwe, there was no escape for him. We know now of many families in our city who have sold their souls to these devils."

Meena asked, "Do you have any idea who it is? His contact here, I mean."

"No. That's the problem. We suspect it is a Zimbabwean."

"Mr and Mrs Munyaradzi, have you met Professor Chikwava?"

"You mean the head of the Department of African Studies? Yes, of course. Ignatius was a TA in the department. Soon after Ignatius began his work here, Professor Chikwava wrote to us praising our son's work ethic and his intelligence. And soon after our arrival here, he came to the hotel to visit. We discovered that our native villages are in the same province — outside of Harare. He is Ndebele, we are Shona. The three official languages of Zimbabwe are Shona, Ndebele, and English. Professor Chikwava had studied Shona in school, as had I Ndebele. We conversed in all three languages!"

Meena suddenly sat up straight.

"Have you kept Ignatius' letter to you? That last letter where he talked about the threat?"

"Why, yes! In fact, I have been carrying it with me the whole time."

Mr Munyaradzi opened his wallet and took out a sheet of paper. Meena looked at the writing. It was in Shona.

"Allow me to translate," Munyaradzi said.

"Respected, beloved parents! I pray that you are both healthy and happy. Your obedient son has thought long and hard before putting pen to paper. I beg your forgiveness for not being more truthful with you. But since your lives are now in jeopardy, I dare not take any chances. Although I told you that I was not being used for drugs, they continue to force me to do so, threatening to kill you, my beloved parents. Father, if you could only leave that godforsaken country and come to the U.S. with my beloved mother! But I imagine that it will remain a dream."

"Did you write back?"

"Yes, I did, at once. In fact, I told him that our attempts to get a temporary visa to come visit him were successful. As a result of the 1992 Land Acquisition Act, I had received compensation for farming land that my ancestors had lost decades before to white farmers. We used the money to bribe a senior official in the Department of the Registrar General in Harare. He assured us that he would try to get us a ten-day visa. We would have to sign a bond that we would return, failing which our lands, everything we owned, would be confiscated, and relatives and friends randomly imprisoned; God only knows what else. We knew what that meant, but our primary concern was our son. I wrote to Ignatius to expect us very soon. How could we know that we would be too late?"

He broke down and wept. His wife cradled his head in her lap and wept too. Meena sat there unable to move. But her mind was racing ahead. *Motive! We have a motive.*

March 27: Motive?

Anthony Chikwava shifted his considerable weight uneasily in the narrow steel chair that was part of the austere furnishings in Chief Inspector Bonnie Martel's office. He was about to get up and look for the chief when she came in with two mugs of coffee.

"I don't know how you take yours, Professor. Here is some cream and sugar."

"Thank you, Chief Inspector. Your sergeant said you wanted to question me, question me about Ignatius Munyaradzi. I have already provided his personal file. Do you have more questions? You understand, my time is precious, time is precious. Your sergeant came to me in the middle, in the middle of a class."

"I apologize for our lack of courtesy, Professor. But the seriousness of the matter left us no other option."

She sipped her coffee silently, watching him like a hawk. He seemed perfectly relaxed, stirred three spoons of sugar into his coffee, and grimaced as he took a sip.

"Are you in the habit, Professor, of calling your students on their cell phones?"

He looked surprised.

"No, of course not! My administrative assistant takes care of such routine matters, such routine matters. Is this important?"

"Yes. Your number appears a dozen times in Ignatius' cell under 'recent calls.'"

"My number? Are you sure?"

"Yes. It is your office number, isn't it?"

"Yes, but... That is impossible! I cannot believe that... I always lock, always lock my door when I'm away. You understand I have confidential files on my faculty in my filing cabinet, my filing cabinet."

Chief Inspector Bonnie Martel put her cup down. Her years of experience studying human expressions would not betray her. His consternation was genuine. But it wouldn't hurt to keep an eye on him, check his background some more.

"Thank you, Professor Chikwava!"

"You are most welcome." He laughed. "Not that those hooligans, those hooligans in my class will miss me! These so-called millennials have no interest, no interest in real education."

March 27: A telephone number rings a bell

The cousins were just washing dishes after an early supper when Chief Inspector Bonnie Martel rang the doorbell. Madhu's teaching schedule had taken her out of the house early in the morning and would keep her busy the whole day. They didn't expect her back until much later. They looked enquiringly at the chief, hoping to hear something promising after her conversation with Professor Chikwava.

"Nothing?"

"Nothing!" Chief Inspector Martel echoed. "You ladies would have come to the same conclusion. He was genuinely surprised... And appalled that I would even suggest such a thing."

"But... But," Leela spluttered. "The number! How could that be?"

She looked at her cousin. Meena stood up, lifted her backpack, and said, "I have an idea. Can we go to the professor's office now, Chief Inspector?"

A puzzled Chief Inspector drove the cousins to the African Studies Department. They saw Professor Chikwava exiting the building.

"Good!" Meena said. "Just what I was hoping for."

They entered the building. Martel knocked on the door that had the name 'Professor Anthony Chikwava' emblazoned across it in gold letters. A petite redhead, possibly in her early forties, opened the door. She looked at them enquiringly.

"Yes? How can I help you? If you need an appointment with Professor Chikwava…"

"No, no. That's all right, Ms…."

"Wrathall, Juliette Wrathall."

"Ms Wrathall, I am Chief Inspector Bonnie Martel. May I come in? It won't take more than a few minutes."

She led her into the office.

"Yes, of course."

She looked with astonishment as Leela and Meena followed the chief into the room. Meena observed her with new interest. *Her accent — it's not British. Australian?*

Martel said, "Ms Wrathall, this is Professor Leela Rao and Ms Meena Rao. They are assisting us in the investigation of the two murders."

"Professor Leela Rao — of course! You are our commencement speaker. It is indeed a pleasure to meet you."

"Ms Wrathall, you've been with the department for some time now, correct?"

"Nine years on the job!"

Meena sat forward in her chair. *Afrikaans — she is from Southern Africa!*

"Tell me, Ms Wrathall, your accent — I'm unable to place it. I hope you don't mind, but may I ask where you're from — originally?"

"Rhodes… I mean Zimbabwe."

I knew it!

"You were about to say Rhodesia! The name Wrathall — wasn't that the name of one of your presidents?"

Wrathall looked at her.

"Your general knowledge is laudable, Ms Rao. Hardly anyone remembers the second president of Rhodesia, even Rhodesians! I am a distant cousin."

Meena continued, "When did you move to the U.S.?"

"1980. I was eighteen when my parents decided to emigrate."

"Wasn't that the year the Republic of Zimbabwe was formed?"

Wrathall nodded. She stood up.

"I don't wish to appear impolite, but should you wish to make an appointment with Professor Chikwava, I would be glad to do so."

"Ms Wrathall," the chief asked, "I assume that you screen all calls made to Professor Chikwava, don't you?"

"Yes. That's part of my job description. Anything else?"

"You must be close to the students in the department."

150

Wrathall looked nonplussed.

"Yes, of course. They come to me for all kinds of things."

She continued more self-confidently, "My responsibilities are wide-ranging, as you can imagine. They include the first contact with students and prospective students. I also maintain student and faculty files. Students come to me for visa information, grades, applications for transcripts."

She stopped what was obviously a well-rehearsed text.

"I... I don't see... Can you tell me what this is about?"

The chief inspector got up.

"Thank you for your time."

She marched the cousins out of the office before they could say anything more. They had hardly got into the chief's car than Leela said, "That was interesting, Chief. What were you getting at with the question about telephone calls? She was distinctly rattled! But why? What did it mean?"

"It meant that she has the same telephone number as her boss. The calls to Ignatius could very well have come from her."

The cousins nodded appreciatively. Leela said, "We have to check her financials. If she is part of the drug ring, it will show up somewhere. Of course, she'll have hidden everything cleverly."

"But why work as a secretary?" Meena thought out aloud, then answered her own question.

"If she is a conduit, then she has positioned herself very well. In an African Studies Department, the comings and goings of Africans wouldn't attract much attention, would it?"

"I see what you mean, Ms Rao," the chief commented. "The Harare-Montpelier connection. No one will suspect her, of course. Moreover, if she is indeed a distant cousin of a prominent Rhodesian family, she must have serious connections and clout."

The chief looked thoughtfully at the cousins.

"You know something, ladies? I'm worried, about your safety, I mean. Ms Rao, your probing questions about her background didn't make the woman happy at all. If she suspects that we are on to her, she will either disappear or resort to violent means to stop you from probing more into her background. Please don't go behind my back from now on! And if you absolutely have to investigate on your own, tell me first what you plan to do."

She dropped the cousins at Madhu's home and drove off with a resigned smile. She knew by now that the cousins would resist any attempt to restrain them.

March 28: An accomplice turns snitch

The cousins looked dejectedly at one another. They weren't used to being kept out of the loop.

"Wish Murali was here. He always allowed us a lot of latitude. Chief Martel hasn't really lost her initial scepticism, has she?"

"No, I suppose not," Meena agreed. "What if we were to push the Wrathall woman over the edge?"

"You mean, set a trap?" Leela asked. "Wow, cousin! You are trumping my own desire to devise sneaky plans!"

"Listen first, you dope! What I'm suggesting is the following."

She called Bonnie Martel. The Chief Inspector listened intently, ended the call, and dialled the U.S. Department of Justice, Tax Division, with an urgent request for Juliette Wrathall's financials. An hour later, the department faxed the report over to her office. Law enforcement agencies had been given limited ability for some time now to obtain financial records concerning foreign accounts in so-called tax havens. Wrathall had apparently always claimed that she did not own any foreign accounts. Martel called her contact at the

Department of Justice and urged him to put the FBI onto Wrathall on suspicion of holding financial interests in the Cayman Islands.

March 28: Things come together

He got out of the private jet. A limousine dropped him off at the Anderson College parking lot where he had left his car. He drove it to his house in the College Hill neighbourhood of Montpelier. A long, hot shower later he lounged on a purple velvet chaise lounge, a Bombay Sapphire martini at his side. He suddenly smiled at a memory. Grabbing the martini, he walked to his briefcase and took out a package. Chanel Coco Mademoiselle — that's what he had smelt on her. He put it back, took out his cell, and punched in a number.

"What? When? Okay, I'll take care of it. I'm meeting her now."

He made himself another martini. Ten minutes later, he parked the car a couple of blocks away from a row of townhouses. It was close to ten p.m. and most of the apartments were dark. He opened the front door and climbed the stairs. The smell of Coco Chanel guided him to her bedroom. The door was open and the familiar voice with its distinct Zimbabwean accent sang out:

"What's the problem? You're usually not strong on proprieties!"

She spilled some of the champagne as she held out a flute to him. *She has had quite a few.* He downed the champagne in one gulp. Then he took the perfume out of the briefcase. Her eyes lit up for a second before glazing over.

"What's wrong?"

"Chief Inspector Bonnie Martel visited me today, asked about telephone calls. She knows something."

"She knows nothing, nothing, do you hear? Don't be an ass! And drink some coffee, for heaven's sake!"

He handed her an envelope of cash and left. A squad car parked in the side alley of a neighbouring building quietly observed his departure. Juliette Wrathall hurriedly got up, placed the cash and a long envelope containing a one-way ticket to Harare in her handbag, dragged a heavy suitcase down the stairs, and went to her car.

***

Madhu had just finished grading the last of twenty-six term papers. She stretched her arms above her head, yawned widely to fill her cramped lungs, and staggered out of her chair. *My kingdom for a hot steaming mug of coffee à la Meena aunty*! Her thoughts went to Charles, as they had been doing quite often since their last meeting. He had been away three days now. Gosh! Was she really falling for the guy? She rewound their last conversation in her head. He had been so considerate, trying to distract her from her preoccupation with the murders. But how could she forget the violence, the beheading — Charles had suggested Al-Qaeda; he had also reminded her of Daniel Pearl.

She entered the grades for the papers into her laptop, shut it down, and slipped it into her briefcase. Al-Qaeda! But now everything pointed to a drug cartel. Meena aunty had called it misdirection. *Wait a minute… How did… No, it wasn't possible, it couldn't be…*

March 28: Denouement

The man drove back to College Hill, went to the closet, and put on a black hoodie, black sweat pants, and a pair of black sneakers. He tucked a gun into his belt and drove back to Wrathall's place.

This time he went to the rear of the building, lifted a window, and slipped into what he knew to be the dining room. Once again, he climbed the stairs to her bedroom. It was open, the room dark. She must have gone to sleep. He stood still for a moment, listening for any signs of sleep. Quiet breathing reached his ears. Good! He entered the room and silently went up to the bed. He could make out her shape under the sheet that she had pulled up all the way to cover her face.

No more trips on a yacht, no more vacations in Monte Carlo, my darling! This is the end of the road for you.

He took out his gun and was about to point it at her head when the lights suddenly came on, blinding him. He whipped his gun around and fired a couple of shots. *What the…*

A voice boomed from the corridor:

"Drop your gun — now! We have you covered. Charles Nozipo Nandoro, you are under arrest on suspicion of drug-trafficking, attempted murder, and first-degree murder!"

Chief Inspector Bonnie Martel entered the room, her gun directed at Nandoro's chest.

"Sergeant Erickson, please read him his rights."

The sergeant stepped forward and intoned, "Charles Nozipo Nandoro, you have the right to remain silent. Anything you say or do can and will be used against you in a court of law. You have the right to an attorney. If you cannot afford an attorney, one will be appointed to you. Do you understand these rights as they have been read to you?"

He ignored Nandoro's curses and quickly handcuffed him. As they walked out, Charles saw Juliette Wrathall similarly handcuffed standing between two FBI agents. He heard a sound behind him and saw Chief Inspector Bonnie Martel pull the bed sheet off a female cop.

March 29: Wrapping things up

Chief Inspector Bonnie Martel was gratified. She had just received a commendation from the commissioner about her work in solving all three homicides. And she was gathering increasing evidence pointing to Charles Nandoro as the arsonist as well. *Superintendent Bonnie Martel! Has a nice ring to it.* Her daydream was shattered by the sound of her cell buzzing.

"Chief Inspector... Oh! Good day, President Juarez. For lunch, sir? I would be very pleased to attend. Thank you, sir!"

President Carlos Juarez greeted the small gathering in the conference room of the administrative building: Chief Inspector Bonnie Martel, Professor Leela Rao, Ms Meena Rao, Assistant Professor Madhu Trivedi, Professor Anthony Chikwava, Martin McDonald, Mr and Mrs Munyaradzi, Mariah Wilson, and Sheila Gilmore.

"Friends, I feel honoured to greet such a wonderful group of people. Thank you for agreeing to meet me at such short notice. You have been instrumental in restoring peace to our community. I would like to acknowledge and thank each and every one of you for your part in this endeavour."

He turned to Bonnie Martel.

"Chief Inspector, Anderson College thank you and the wonderful officers of our police department for your service."

Martel blushed with pleasure.

"President Juarez, it's our duty. We are committed to protecting our community. But I couldn't have achieved results so quickly without the invaluable help of a few friends."

She turned to the cousins.

"Professor Leela Rao, Mrs Meena Rao — the police department owes you an immense debt of gratitude for making sense of all the leads we had. What did you call it, Mrs Meena Rao? Misdirection! Yes, indeed! You quickly got us out of falling into the easy trap of blaming the entire Islamic world!"

She turned to Professor Chikwava.

"Professor, my sincere apologies once again to you for dragging you into all this. If I had only guessed…"

Chikwava mumbled, "No harm done, dear lady, no harm done. Under the circumstances quite understandable, quite understandable."

Martel continued, "We now know that you and Mr and Mrs Munyaradzi and several other Zimbabweans have been fighting crime in your country and trying to stop the inhuman practice of using the bodies of young men and women to smuggle life-threatening drugs."

Mr Munyaradzi nodded.

"Yes. We formed an oppositional group years ago to fight Mugabe's tyranny and corruption. Professor Chikwava played a major role in identifying such abuse and saving as many of our children as possible. We have a long way to go — the drug cartels have the money to bribe our government officials. But we will continue to fight them."

President Juarez looked at the cousins.

"Professor Rao, we will have the pleasure of greeting you again in a couple of months. But I am curious about something. When did you begin to suspect Charles Nandoro?"

Leela said, looking slyly at Meena, "It was actually my partner in crime, my cousin Meena. She recognized that the murders had been staged to point a finger at Islamist terrorists — Chief Inspector Martel told you about it already — 'misdirection'. I was guilty of having similar suspicions. Your student Abdelkarim al-Adel seemed to fit the profile for O'Flaherty's killing, but not for Ignatius'. And Madhu's — Professor Trivedi's realization that Nandoro knew more about the murders than what the police had released to the press was a clincher. Madhu?"

"Nandoro mentioned ritual and beheading. How could he have known about it? Chief Inspector Martel had issued a gag order to us and his department about the beheading and the calligraphy," Madhu explained. "I should have been more vigilant. And seeing that sports car in the parking garage — that should have raised a red flag."

"Don't blame yourself, Professor Trivedi," Martel consoled. "The man was smooth… And very charming."

Madhu cringed and muttered under her breath, "That he was, the bastard!"

Meena pressed her hand comfortingly.

Chief Inspector Martel continued, "Nandoro used his McMoran connections and money to forge alliances with international drug trafficking syndicates. Zimbabwe has serious deficiencies in its criminal justice system. Nandoro made periodic visits to the various hubs that included drugs and arms trafficking. Airports in Ethiopia and Kenya have connections between West Africa and the heroin-producing countries in South West and South East Asia. The volume of cocaine that police have seized in Africa is still relatively small, but criminals like Nandoro are bound to extend their highly-organized networks to change this. Nandoro also dealt in counterfeit medicines, especially with India."

Juarez shook his head.

"Forgive my ignorance, but if Nandoro was using O'Flaherty as a drug mule, why kill him? O'Flaherty was obviously making tons of money for him and for himself."

"I think I can answer that, President Juarez," Chief Inspector Martel responded. "In checking his computer

163

records, we found out that he started skimming off the top. Bank deposits didn't show anything noticeable at first. But then we noticed hundreds of dollars, then thousands. He thought Nandoro wouldn't find out."

"Greed got him killed. Why did Nandoro and his gang choose Anderson College?" Juarez wondered.

Mrs Munyaradzi spoke up, "Mr President, rich colleges in the U.S., such as yours, are increasingly being targeted by our drug dealers. They take advantage of the fact that some of us parents are willing to pay any price to get our children out of Zimbabwe to a safe country."

Mr Munyaradzi added, "My wife is actually talking about us. We fell prey to the very inhumanity that we are now vigorously fighting. We had been desperately looking for ways to get our son out of the country. One day, a contact approached us wanting to use our Ignatius as a drug mule in return for safe, free passage to the U.S. He assured us that this was a one-time deal, that they wouldn't make any further demands on Ignatius once he had transported the drugs. How could we have been so naïve as to believe that criminals like that could have even a shred of integrity or humanity?"

The couple looked at Martin McDonald with tears in their eyes. He stood up.

"I have a request. My parents-in-law and I are celebrating Ignatius' union with Muwari, the impersonal, omnipotent Creator in whom the Shona believe. Muwari is a spirit that creates good and bad."

He looked at the Munyaradzis for confirmation, then continued, "Chief Inspector Martel and the Medical Examiner were gracious enough to return Ignatius to us as we knew him in life."

He turned to Mrs Munyaradzis.

"Mother, would you…"

Mrs Munyaradzis nodded.

"We would be happy if you would join us in preparing our Ignatius so that he may be accepted by our ancestors. You will be our witnesses when we ritually bathe and anoint him so that he may 'leave all the dirt of the world = chisiya svina yose yapasi'."

Leela said, "We will bring tokens of sympathy to wish him a speedy transmigration."

The Munyaradzis folded their hands in appreciation. Mrs Munyaradzi said, "Professor Rao, with elders such as you to bless him, our son will surely look after us well, as all our dearly departed do. After cleansing his body, we will cremate him in deference to his and our son Martin's Buddhist beliefs."

"Yes," Martin added. "We will remove the arrow."

Epilogue

483 BCE, Kushinagar, India: Remove the arrow

…the slings and arrows
of outrageous fortune.

The Blessed One lay on a low cot, his frail body wracked with pain. His cousin and companion Ananda sat at the foot, gently massaging his master's feet.

The Buddha whispered, "Do you know, Ananda, what I asked my father before I left the palace? Whether I would also fall down on the ground and become as cold as stone if Pasenadi were to shoot an arrow into me."

Ananda broke down and wept uncontrollably.

"Ananda, Ananda, my friend! Listen! I am frail now, Ananda, old, aged, far gone in years. This is my eightieth year, and my life is spent. My body is like an old cart, barely held together.[15] Therefore, Ananda, be an island unto yourself, a refuge unto yourself, seeking

---

15

http://buddhism.about.com/od/buddha/a/parinirvana.htm Accessed: October 6, 2019.

no other refuge; with the Dharma as your island, the Dharma as your refuge, seeking no other refuge."

They heard sounds of sorrow outside. A group of monks entered the hut. Mahakassapa, one of the Buddha's most trusted Bhikkhus, fell to his knees in front of the Blessed One.

"Master, we believe it was Pasenadi's low-caste son Vidudabha, the new king of Kosala, who colluded with the people who call themselves Jains and allowed them to hire assassins. They murdered our beloved Moggallana because they wish to curtail your fame. And now they have destroyed your body as well."

The Buddha raised his head to look into Ananda's eyes. He wondered why Ananda had not been targeted. Moggallana was his senior-most disciple. But it was Ananda who had memorized all his teachings.

"Master!" he heard Ananda's anguished cry. "Why? Why is this happening? Why did you not keep him safe? You are Gautama, you are the Buddha! For twenty-five years, I have served you without question.

Through a full 25 years
As long as I have been in higher training
I have never had a thought of lust:
See, how powerfully the Dhamma works.[16]

16

http://www.accesstoinsight.org/lib/authors/hecker/wheel27 3.html#section-1 Accessed: October 6, 2019

Lord! You are the Buddha, the Sublime Teacher. How is it that you allowed this heinous crime to take place?"

The Buddha looked with great sorrow at his friend and the other monks who had gathered in the hut.

"Bhikkhus! In one of his past births, Moggallana had done a great wrong to his own parents, who were both blind: In the beginning, he was a very dutiful son. But after his marriage, his wife began to make trouble and suggested that he should get rid of his parents. He took his blind parents in a cart into a forest. And there he killed them by beating them and making them believe that it was some thief who was beating them. For that evil deed, he suffered in niraya[17] for a long time. And in this birth, his last, he has died at the hands of assassins. Indeed, by doing wrong to those who should not be wronged, one is sure to suffer for it."[18]

He paused and breathed deeply.

*"Ananda, my cousin, my friend, perform this one last service for me. I have carried it in my heart all these years. **Remove the arrow.**"*

---

[17] "Hell," "hell realm," or "purgatory" in Pāli
[18] *http://wisdomquarterly.blogspot.com/2009/12/killing-of-maha-moggallana.html Accessed: October 6, 2019.*